Operation Arctic

Leif Hamre

Operation Arctic

Translated from the Norwegian by Dag Ryen

A MARGARET K. MC ELDERRY BOOK

ATHENEUM *1973* NEW YORK

Contents

Operation Arctic

The Air Base

Andøya, like so many of the islands in northern Norway, stands naked before the open sea. The weather can be cruel, especially during the long and dark winter. When blizzards rage at their worst, stretching icy fingers over the endless, barren marshes, people must stay indoors to survive. Were it not for the sheltering mountain range that divides the island from north to south, life would have been unbearable for the islanders. But that rough, towering barrier makes all the difference. It shelters the inhabitants of the western slopes from the north-easterly polar winds and screens their eastern neighbours from the salt-sprayed gales that roll in from the sea. Nature's benefits and hardships are thus meted out in a just and equitable manner.

There is a little fishing village on the northern tip of the island called Andenes. For many years it was a peaceful and quiet place, somewhat shut off from the outside world. Village life revolved around the harbour. In fair weather the fishing boats would slip out through the breakwater in the grey light of dawn, returning later in the day with their catches. While shorebound, the fishermen would linger on the quay exchanging local gossip or private thoughts on world matters, measuring the sky with squinted eyes and chewing meditatively on the stems of their pipes.

The air base brought a new era to the island. First came the people from the Air Force who tramped around the marshes for no apparent reason. Then surveyors followed with their transits and measuring tapes, and finally the construction workers poured in. Soon the streets and alleys of the quiet village were filled with a noisy bustle.

Boatload after boatload of building materials were unloaded at the quay and jetty. Trucks crawled day and night along the winding roads. Bulldozers traversed the marshes shifting turf and wet earth. A rumbling stamp mill chewed boulders from the nearby mountains, and spat out gravel and broken stone.

The hordes of newcomers were extremely busy. For a while the islanders took the flurry of activity with stoic calm. Then little by little they were caught up in the seething whirlpool. More houses were needed, more schools, more shops, more cafés, more filling stations. Money began to circulate and passed quickly from hand to hand.

Meanwhile the air base gradually took shape. The marshes were drained and graded. Runways were gravelled and covered with concrete. Hangars rose like giant skeletons and were clothed in metal sheets. Houses, large

4

and small, shot up like mushrooms after rain, and new roads criss-crossed the moors like spiderwebs.

The Air Force quarters were built where the mountainsides slope down to the Skarstein Valley. With barracks, messes and offices, a small church, a hospital and ample sports facilities, the little community could compare favourably with a small village. A few miles away, on the outskirts of Andenes, a new residential area was under construction. The houses were laid out in uniform, monotonous rows between the seashore and the highway at a place called Merket.

When the base was finally ready to receive a squadron of maritime patrol aircraft, more than five hundred men had already been transferred to the base quarters in the Skarstein Valley, and the married servicemen had found new homes for their families at Merket. Most of them had children, youngsters whose speech sparkled with dialects from all corners of the country, harsh and soft, monotone and musical, energetic and slow. Their voices intertwined in Babylonian confusion.

Most of the youngsters had known Air Force life from birth and were accustomed to a nomadic existence. They had lived at other camps and bases where the rows of houses were just like those at Merket. Only the weather and the neighbours differed. Many of the children adapted quickly to the changes and soon made new friends. For others the transition was more difficult. They could not seem to forget the friends they had left behind, and had trouble making new ones.

The construction workers and machines disappeared. Planes replaced them. The quiet peacefulness that once lingered over Andenes was gone for ever. The chugging of the fishing boats as they headed out to sea at dawn was lost in the roar of aircraft engines. Even the raucous squabbling of the gulls over scraps thrown overboard by the fishermen as they cleaned their catch seemed to have lost its edge.

It was a school holiday.

The children at Merket were nonetheless up and about early, braving the wet and uninviting autumn weather. A holiday provided a welcome opportunity to do things they had daydreamed about while staring out of classroom windows. Field hockey, which filled the gap between soccer and ice hockey seasons, was the current rage. The soccer field had long been too wet and sloppy, and the ponds and lakes were still free of ice. But field hockey had the advantage that it could be played almost anywhere. A strip of lawn between the houses was all they needed. Ice or grass—the excitement was the same and the field version provided good training for the skating season just around the corner.

Some of the children had to content themselves with watching. The girls, except for a few who were as strong as any of the boys, were overlooked when sides were chosen.

So were the youngsters under ten years old. They acted as cheerleaders or passed the time by building dams and river-beds in the dirt road that led to the main highway. Very few of the others were found unworthy of a place on one of the teams. But there were some.

Torgeir Solheim was one of them. He was too skinny and weak to be of any use so long as there were others to choose from. They called him Midge, not because of his size—he was certainly tall enough—but because he simply lacked muscle and courage. Anybody could tackle him by meeting him straight on. He would shy away, giving up the ball with little or no effort.

Arne Halvorsen was also a spectator, surprisingly enough from the looks of him. He was strong enough if anyone was—a little short perhaps, but stoutly built and with a round, self-satisfied face and large, irregular teeth.

But no one wanted him on their side. Teamwork and team spirit were things he couldn't get into his head. What he understood by hockey was a series of brutal tackles from which his own team suffered about as much as the opponents.

The game began as usual with a chorus of shouts and cries, mostly from the players. The spectators weren't nearly as enthusiastic, and Torgeir and Arne were practically silent. Yet, at one point or another, as they leaned against their hockey sticks, pretending to be indifferent to the entire game, a word or sentence dropped between them and was misunderstood.

It was really nothing more than a triviality. Nonetheless, Arne's temper flared and he grabbed Torgeir by the arm.

"Want to make something of it?" he asked.

"Me? No." Torgeir backed off and bumped into the wall of a building. Arne followed after him.

"What ya say then, Midge? Huh?"

"Nothing. Nothing to you."

"Oh, no? Somethin' about me, maybe?"

"No." Torgeir shook his head.

"Ain't got guts enough to stand up for it, huh?" Arne lowered his head a bit and stood on guard with his fists clenched.

As always when a fight was brewing, a flock of youngsters seemed to pop up from nowhere and crowd around them.

Torgeir pressed himself flat against the building. His windbreaker was too big and fell in large folds from his narrow shoulders. The tufts of hair that peeked out from under his cap were blond, and his pointed and rather weak face was pale. Blue-grey shadows underlined his eyes.

"Don't dare defend yourself, either?" goaded Arne.

Torgeir didn't answer. He held one arm about chin high as his eyes darted nervously from Arne to the steadily growing crowd of kids. Someone or other yelled in a thin voice: "Clobber him, then he'll have to."

The crowd pressed closer and began to scream in chorus to egg them on. It sounded like a long, drawn-out E.

"E-e-e-e-e! E-e-e-e-e!"

Accompanied by drums it might just as well have been the ritual song to a tribal dance.

Only two of the kids in the crowd, a set of twins, were quiet. They were Torgeir's brother and sister, just past their eighth birthday. The way they were dressed, both with knitted caps, windbreakers, pants and rubber boots, made it difficult to tell which was which. Lise paid no heed to the likeness, but Terje lit up like a firecracker when somebody mistook the one for the other. He kept his straw-yellow hair cut short, and demanded that Lise let her curls grow. But the sky-blue eyes, the straight nose

8

and the full mouth were carbon copies. No one could change that.

Torgeir wished the twins hadn't been there. He tried to get out of the trap by taking a step to one side. But it was no use. The first blow caught him on the forearm. The back of his head banged against the wall, and he unwittingly let his guard drop and caught the next one across the mouth. He felt the salty taste of blood on his lips.

"Gee," said Lise. She grabbed Terje by the arm to pull him out of the crowd, but he resisted, and they remained standing.

"I haven't done a thing to you," Torgeir appealed to Arne. "I don't know why we're fighting."

"Are you fighting?" Arne grinned. "I hadn't noticed."

The crowd had quietened down to catch what was being said.

"You'd better give up, then," Arne offered, generously.

Torgeir looked around uncertainly in the faint hope that some adult would come along and break up the fight. That had happened before, but now there was no one in sight. People stayed indoors out of the drizzling rain.

A moment's uneasiness swept through the crowd. Someone had shoved the twins aside so they couldn't see, but Terje crawled between the legs of those in front of him until he suddenly cropped up beside Arne.

"He's not scared of you," he shouted loudly and angrily.

"Shut up, squirt," Arne said. "Nobody asked you." He glanced haughtily, but also with some surprise, at the little firebrand staring straight into his face.

"Outa the way," he said, shoving the youngster aside.

9

Terje tripped over his own feet. He flailed with his arms to regain balance. His eyes nearly popped out of his head as he appealed to Torgeir: "He pushed me! Didya see he pushed me!"

Torgeir decided he had no choice. He threw himself forward and wrapped his arms around Arne's head. They tumbled together to the sloppy ground.

Arne frothed: "Idiot, you're messin' up my clothes."

They rolled around and Arne came out on top. The crowd was squealing with glee. Torgeir clutched at Arne to block the blows. But he lost his hold. Arne squirmed free and sat astride his stomach, lifting a threatening fist in the air.

"Give up," he shouted, enraged.

No one noticed Terje grab the hockey stick that Torgeir had dropped. Deliberately, but without haste, he moved up to the combatants, lifted the stick in the air, took aim calmly at the back of Arne's head, and swung with all his might.

Arne crumpled and fell to one side into the mud. He lay perfectly still, blood streaming from a cut in his head.

"Oh, geeeeee," stuttered Lise, who had also worked her way to the front of the crowd. She covered her mouth with one hand as if to muffle a scream.

Torgeir crawled to his knees. He gaped in disbelief at the motionless figure beside him. It began to dawn on him what had happened when he saw Terje with the hockey stick in his hands, fighting back the tears.

The crowd dispersed. Some ran. Others retreated step by step as if they couldn't quite tear themselves away. A voice at some distance shouted hysterically to those running by, "He's . . . get some grownups . . . he's killed him."

At that moment Terje fled. His short legs churned like pistons in his huge rubber boots. He fell as he crossed the lawn. He fell again as he rounded the corner of a house. Then he was out of sight.

"Come on," Torgeir said to Lise. The last thing he noticed before he ran off was that Arne rolled over and moaned. At least he was alive. But Torgeir hadn't time to look closer. He took Lise by the hand and set off after Terje. On reaching the corner of the house they saw him cross the highway and scamper for dear life across the fields towards the dried-out marshes where no one lived.

They didn't catch up with him until he halted in front of the fence surrounding the airport. By then they were all exhausted and gasping for air. They walked on slowly until they found a small shed that had once been used to store dried turf. Some beams and a ragged roof were all that was left of the place, but it provided a semblance of shelter from the drizzle. They went in and sat down on the stacks of turf. From beyond a small hill nearby, they could hear the drone of an aircraft engine.

Torgeir gnawed at a fingernail. It bled a little because there was almost nothing left to bite on. His nails were always chewed to the roots.

After a long silence he said thoughtfully, "He moved."

"Who?" asked Lise.

"Arne."

"I—I didn't hit him hard," stammered Terje. He was having trouble sitting still.

Torgeir did not look up. He kicked at a piece of moist turf at his feet, studying it closely. After a while he spoke: "He was bleedin' somethin' fierce, though. Afraid he got an awful hole in his head."

"Might have been a knot in the stick," said Terje. "He lost his cap. I couldn't help it."

"Help what?"

"That he lost his cap. That's why he got a hole in his head. You think anyone's searching for us?"

"Not yet. They're probably busy getting Arne to the hospital. Why'd you clobber him?"

"He was trying to murder you. And he called you Midge." Terje lifted his head and listened. "The motor has stopped," he said divertingly. "Will they have to stitch it up?"

"Stitch?"

"Yeah, his head."

Torgeir carefully probed his bloodied lip. It was sore.

"They usually do. Sew up head cuts, I mean."

"They'll have to shave him, then," said Terje. He shifted nervously. "He'll look like Andersen at the grocery store. Andersen got so fierce, his head grew right *through* his hair. Since then he only has a beard and nothing on top."

"Pooh," said Lise, pressing her nose flat with one finger and raising her eyes. Such gestures were her way of expressing an opinion.

"That's a bunch of baloney that somebody's made up," said Torgeir. "Besides, they'll just shave him on a small spot. Andersen's bald on his whole head."

"That's why he has so much beard," maintained Terje.

"He has to drink through a straw. He has a sawed-off bicycle pump that he pumps in soup with."

"Rubbish," said Torgeir. "Whoever told you that?"

"A boy in my class. He *knows*, 'cause he *knows* Andersen. I guess somebody'll soon come and find us. We'll get a whipping." Terje rubbed his bottom.

"Not me," said Lise.

"Why not?"

"'Cause I'm a girl."

"That doesn't mean you don't have a bottom, too."

"But I haven't done anything," Lise exclaimed, raising her voice. "I wasn't a part of it. I *wasn't*!"

Terje looked at her sourly. Then, unwillingly, he accepted her arguments. "I don't want to go home," he said. "And I won't go to school tomorrow."

The others didn't answer. Their mood had hit rock bottom.

"Anyway, I'm sick," declared Terje. "When I've stayed out all night, I'll be even more sick! And I *hate* school!"

The Aircraft

The rain had stopped, but the children remained in the shed, not knowing where else to go.

"We could go and look at the planes," Terje suggested.

Torgeir thought for a moment. "Better not," he said. "Somebody may have heard that they're searching for us."

The argument was weighty enough, but Lise wasn't satisfied.

"We can't just sit here all night," she said. "I'm going home, even if nobody else is." Still, she made no move to carry out the threat.

"I'd go home, too, if Dad were there," Terje sighed.

"He might come." Torgeir looked up anxiously as if he expected to see an aircraft overhead. "Mum will certainly call Sola to tell Dad what happened. Maybe he'll come."

"When he learns that we've run away," said Terje, optimistically.

"Mmmm." Torgeir seemed to brighten a bit at the thought. "We can wait till we see a plane arrive from Sola," he said.

"How can we tell that?" Lise looked at Torgeir with blue, uncomprehending eyes. Her face was framed by the hood of her red jacket. With her hair hidden underneath it she could be either one of the twins except for the colour of the windbreaker. Terje's jacket was blue.

"You can tell by—"

Torgeir was interrupted by Terje who drowned out his brother's voice.

"Don't you know? All you have to do is read the letters on the fuselage. At Sola they begin with W and H. At Andøya they read KK and something, like KKA or KKB. Don't you *know* that?"

Lise tossed her head. "Don't care to know, either," she retorted.

Terje didn't listen. He continued undaunted. "Dad's plane had KKG when he was here. Now he has WHB. That's because he's moved to Sola."

"It's just silly that planes are called anything at all," said Lise sourly. "Why can't Dad be at home?"

"'Cause he's got a new job," said Torgeir. "He's deputy commander of 330 Squadron now."

"Well, how come he can't stay here all the same?"

"Good grief!" Terje sighed. "330 Squadron is at Sola, that's why."

"Captain Henriksen is the deputy commander of 333 Squadron here," Torgeir explained. "So Dad can't be."

"But I wanna *move*!" Lise was so irritated by the flood

of knowledge that she almost shouted. "Why don't we get an apartment at Sola?"

"We will soon," Torgeir said patiently. "But since there are so many of us, Mum and Dad want a big place, so we have to wait till something big enough is available. Dad'll call for us as soon as he gets one."

"I can't see why he has to be a deputy commander," said Lise. "What is a deputy commander anyway?" She knew next to nothing about the Air Force.

"Then he can command his deputies," said Terje.

Torgeir's patience remained firm, his tone of voice barely altered. "He's second in command of the squadron," he corrected gently.

It had become too chilly to sit still. Besides, Terje had stayed in one place a good bit longer than he usually had the patience for. He stood up and glanced warily around for pursuers. His cap was pulled down across his forehead, a habit he had picked up to emphasize the difference between him and Lise.

"Why don't we go and take a look at the planes," he said. "If somebody tries to get us, we can run for it."

Torgeir remained seated. "Can't get past the guards," he said.

"I know of a place where we can crawl under the fence," said Terje, pointing out a direction. "There's a hole in the ground there."

Finally Torgeir gave in and let Terje lead the way. They found the hole and crawled through. Once inside they passed a low hill and walked down a slope to the squadron area. Crossing the road behind the parachute shed they sneaked up to the wall and peered around the corner towards the hangars. In front of one of them stood an Albatross.

They hesitated, reluctant to go further.

"It looks like a boat with wings," Lise observed. "It's got a keel and portholes."

"A seaplane has to have a keel and portholes," Terje asserted. "It can land on water when they pull in the wheels."

"I *know* that," Lise said. "Who's that standing on the stepladder?"

"Can't remember his name," said Terje. "But I know who he is."

"You've seen him at Merket," said Torgeir. "He lives there. I think his name is Myrmo."

Once they felt assured that no one else was nearby, they walked across the apron and assembled in a group in front of the stepladder on which Flight Sergeant Myrmo balanced while tinkering with an engine.

"Hi," he said, glancing down at them between the propeller blades. "Skipping school?" he asked.

"We have the day off," said Torgeir.

"Aha. Congratulations. I don't keep up with those things. My kids are too young for school yet. How did you get past the guards?"

Terje announced: "We know 'bout a hole in the fence."

Myrmo had a funny, birdlike sort of face. He squinted smilingly down at them. "Better get out the same way, then," he said. "I'll be testing these engines in a while. You'll have to be far away when I start up."

They nodded in agreement.

"If you get too close, you'll be swept in by the suction," he added.

They nodded again.

"Happens fast as lightning. Whoosh—you go straight through the propeller and get hacked up into twenty-four pieces."

Lise's hands rose to her mouth. "Why exactly twenty-four?" she asked through her fingers.

"Can't remember," Myrmo said. "It's mathematics, but it's quite a while since I worked it out."

They stood in silence.

Torgeir nodded towards the engine and casually placed one hand in his trouser pocket.

"Is she O.K.?" he asked.

"Looks all right." Myrmo laughed. "But she's a trifle tired, poor thing. This aircraft has flown so far that we have to run her down to Sola today for a complete overhaul."

"When? When's it leaving?"

"Ten this morning."

Lise blurted out: "Can we come along?"

"Want to visit your dad, Dolly?"

"Uh-huh."

"Well, maybe it's not as impossible as it sounds. We're coming back this afternoon with another aircraft that's been overhauled."

"Can we? Huh?"

"I'm not the one to decide. Run on home and ask your mum. If she calls the base commander, chances are he'll say it's O.K. We've got room enough for the lot of you."

Myrmo climbed down the ladder and pulled it over to

the hangar. He turned towards the youngsters and shooed them away.

"Off you go, kids," he called. "Far away. I'm about to start the engines."

They ran off quickly. But Torgeir and Terje slowed down as they reached the parachute shed and stopped behind it. Lise wanted to go on.

"We must hurry," she said.

"Why?"

"If we're gonna ask Mum."

"Oh—no." Torgeir sat down on a rock beside the road. He brushed Lise's suggestion aside. "Whatever makes you think she'll let us go, after what Terje has done. She's probably mad as a hornet."

Lise gave in without another word. It was obvious that Torgeir was right. They heard the engines start and run at idling speed for a while. Then the noise increased to a deafening roar that made it difficult to talk together. The vibrating air tickled their eardrums.

For want of something better to do, Lise began to jump across a ditch beside the road.

"It means good luck if I can do it twenty times without falling in," she explained to Terje.

"What kinda luck?"

"I'll win a lottery or something."

"Do you have a ticket?"

"I can buy one, can't I?"

Terje decided on twenty jumps, too. There was no use missing out on a little luck if that was all there was to it. So far the day hadn't offered much else to write home about.

The sun came out for a while, spreading a little warmth. Clouds were drifting across the entire sky, but patches of blue appeared in between. The rain had stopped completely.

The twins grew short of breath from jumping. They squatted on the grass in front of Torgeir. Lise untied the hood of her windbreaker, took off her cap and shook out her golden curls. They reached below her shoulders.

The roar from behind the shed continued to increase. The whine of the propellers resounded against the wall of the nearest hangar. They had to shout to be heard.

Torgeir tossed aside a stick with which he had been poking absentmindedly in the dirt.

"We could sneak into the plane and hide," he pronounced loudly.

"Do you think we could?"

The twins' enthusiasm was spontaneous. They jumped up as if prepared to put words into action at once. Their response took Torgeir somewhat by surprise. He hadn't expected to be taken literally, without a single reservation. The whole idea was mostly wishful thinking. He just wanted to play with the thought and pretend. To actually do it was something else again.

Terje asked: "Where would we hide? Under the bunk?" He paused expectantly, then added, "There is a bunk in the back of the cabin, you know. The crew use it for a nap on long flights."

"I know." Torgeir knit his brows in thought. "But I'm afraid you're too little. You wouldn't be able to lie still that long."

"Pooh! Yes we can."

Their eyes shone with excitement. At last they had found a ray of light in the otherwise grey and hopeless day. To see Dad was the magic formula that could solve all problems.

Torgeir chewed his lip. He should have bitten his tongue a little earlier instead, hard enough to keep the foolhardy words from slipping out. Now he searched feverishly for a plausible excuse to back out.

"Mum will worry when she can't find us," he said.

It was a rather heedless remark. Terje had no trouble dismissing the objection.

"We're not going home now, anyway," he said, astonished. "Least, that's what you said. Besides, Dad can call home and tell Mum when we get to Sola."

Torgeir was swept by a strong feeling that he was about to lose face for the second time in one day.

"Can you lie perfectly still for almost three hours?" he then asked.

They nodded eagerly.

"Without squirming, talking or coughing?"

"But—but what would it matter? Nobody could hear us anyway as long as the engines are running." Impatience welled up in Terje's eyes that so far had met Torgeir's gaze with eager encouragement. Now the spark started to die out. He turned away and stared moodily at a fixed point on the ground.

"I think you're scared," he said.

His words were barely audible above the noisy engines. But Torgeir more or less read the words on his lips.

"Scared?" he shouted, his eyebrows arching towards

his hairline. "Me, scared? Wasn't it me who thought of the idea?"

The roar of the engines stopped as if cut off by a knife. Torgeir's voice was caught hanging in the air and seemed suddenly high and whining. He paused to listen to two voices shouting in the distance. The hangar doors squeaked. A tractor stood somewhere, sputtering.

When he looked at the twins again, there was expectation in their eyes once more. By now they believed that he dared, believed that he would. It was then he realized that he had to.

After the decision was made, everything went so smoothly that there was no opportunity to turn back. Torgeir wanted to be discovered and did nothing to prevent it. But no one saw them. They walked across the apron, climbed the ladder and got aboard. The plane was empty. They spread a blanket out under the bunk and rolled another into a pillow. Then they crawled in and lay quietly for a while without hearing the slightest noise outside.

Terje lay farthest in. He was the only one to speak. He leaned across Lise and whispered in Torgeir's ear: "If you'd wanted to, I bet you could've knocked his teeth in, easy as pie."

The Island

Captain Bjørn Henriksen draped his uniform jacket on a coat hanger. He pulled on his blue flight suit while whistling a monotonous melody through his teeth, a few phrases over and over again. His compact figure seemed somewhat bulky in the loose overalls. He was of average height. His face was round and jovial and frequent smiles had etched deep wrinkles around his eyes.

Voices buzzed around him. The dressing-room was rather cramped when two crews were changing at the same time. But this morning they had to. Two aircraft were scheduled for take-off at ten o'clock. Lieutenant Berge would be heading south for Sola airport while he himself was going north to Half Moon Island at Svalbard to pick up a sick trapper. The pilot of a commercial aircraft on a routine mail-dropping run over the area had discovered a message marked out on the ground with logs and pieces of driftwood. It read: SOS ILL. The trapper had stumbled out of the cabin, waving frantically. However, the charter aircraft wasn't built for landing on water, and the pilot could do nothing but drop a note in which he promised to notify the Air Force.

When Captain Henriksen had finished changing, he shut the locker door and dropped the key in his pocket.

"You about ready?" he asked a rangy, thin fellow who had the next locker. He wore a navigator's wing and was a second lieutenant.

"Two winks," said the navigator.

"I'll wait." Henriksen leaned against the locker and listened to a shrill voice that cut through the general hubbub from the inner depths of the room.

"Get the lead out, Per—and get that boot on. You afraid there's a snake in it?"

"Can't see none," came the calm reply in the ringing dialect of the town of Bergen. "Less'n he's in the toe. But then, don't recall havin' heard of no vipers north of Salt Mountain."

"Never know—when even Bergeners find their way up here."

"Well now, you got somethin' there. Us Bergen folks's gotta see for ourselves how the outside world suffers so's we can 'preciate our own good fortune once't we're safe back home. Don't know about snakes though."

The navigator, Second Lieutenant Haugen, got ready and followed Captain Henriksen outside. The sun peeked through a break in the clouds, but the air was chilly. September's last days brought autumn to a close as far north as Andøya. The bright colours that had decorated the hillsides below Endleton and Trolltind Mountains were already fading, and the cloudberry plants in the far-stretching marshes were not nearly as red as they had been just a few weeks earlier. South of the Andsfjord the highest peaks were already capped with snow.

Haugen skipped a stride to get in step with Henriksen.

"Good flying weather," he remarked. "Both here and up north. But how do you expect we'll get ashore after we land? The weather report indicates pretty high surf."

"We'll probably find a sheltered sound somewhere." Henriksen had a deep bass voice. "If the worst comes to the worst we'll anchor the plane and row in with the dinghy."

"Won't get much of the trapper's equipment with us, then."

"I know, but we've only got room for a fraction of it anyway. Just imagine the lot he needs to survive through a whole winter. To be on the safe side, in case the pack ice doesn't break up in the summer, he even has to have food and fuel for two seasons. He can never be sure when a ship can reach him and take him home. I reckon we'll just have to pick out the bare essentials and bring them along."

Their Albatross was parked in front of the hangar. They said "hi" to the flight engineer who had finished test-running the engines and was waiting for them with the checklist ready. He went along with Henriksen on the preflight inspection of the fuselage while Haugen climbed the ladder and went aboard.

The other aircraft, bound for Sola, had been moved further down the apron. Flight Sergeant Myrmo had taxied it away from the hangar before shutting down the engines after warm-up.

By the time Henriksen and the flight engineer were ready to go aboard, the rest of the crew had arrived. They scrambled up the ladder and over the doorstep in their huge flight boots, pausing to hang their chutes on hooks before taking their seats. A noisy bustle filled the cabin—murmuring, chattering, coughing, shuffling feet and creaking seats, rustling paper and snapping switches. In time, as each one got his things in order, it became quieter. The flight engineer hauled in the ladder and closed the heavy, sliding door.

Captain Henriksen fastened his seatbelt and put on the headphones. His co-pilot, Lieutenant Strande, pushed the side window open. He nodded to the mechanic who stood ready to plug in the external starter unit.

"Read the checklist," said Henriksen.

Strande read. His finger moved from point to point on a green plastic-coated sheet. They pushed buttons, flicked switches, and shoved levers into position. In the meantime the rest of the crew checked their own gear. Small lights lit up and went out. Meter hands moved. Buzzing and muffled crackling lingered in the air.

"Ready to start starboard engine."

At a sign from Henriksen, a mechanic who was waiting in front of the aircraft moved closer with his fire extinguisher. The starter hummed. Outside the co-pilot's window the propeller ticked slowly over. The engine caught, coughed, caught again. The sudden whine of the propeller came roaring through the open window and Strande hurried to close it. When the second engine had come to life and joined in the rhythm of the first, Captain Henriksen threw a glance towards Lieutenant Berge's plane. It seemed ready to go too; the propellers were turning. Berge met his gaze, from a distance, and turned thumbs up. At the same time his low voice could be heard in the earphones. "You go ahead. I'll follow."

Henriksen shoved the mike in front of his lips and thumbed the transmitter button. "Andøya tower, this is Albatross Kilo Kilo Golf. Good morning. Ready to taxi. Over."

His hand darted to the volume control when the flight controller's distinct voice made the earphones crackle.

"Kilo Kilo Golf from tower. Morning. You are cleared to runway one five. The wind is west at seven knots. Altimeter two nine point nine five inches."

They taxied out to the northern end of the runway and Captain Henriksen released the full power of his engines. The Albatross ate its way down the wide runway, steadily picking up speed. The drumming of the wheels against the concrete became weaker and weaker. The airspeed indicator jerked. The fuselage stopped vibrating, and KKG was in the air.

They banked onto course when the altimeter passed five hundred feet. Underneath they could see KKB crawling down the runway and lifting off. Ahead of them stretched the sea. The horizon was undisturbed to the north and west, but the rugged coastline to starboard was partly hidden in banks of fog.

During the first minutes of flight everyone was busy at their jobs. The pilots scanned the instruments to make sure everything was in perfect shape for the long haul. The radio operator established contact with the maritime operations room from which orders for the continuing flight would come. The navigator bowed his hairless head over the charts. His greatest worry in life was his thinning blond locks. He therefore kept what was left cropped close, having heard it would grow back thicker that way.

The pencil lines that Second Lieutenant Haugen drew on his chart from time to time stretched farther and farther from Andøya. To anyone who was not in on the secrets of navigation, the plotted pattern would have seemed quite incomprehensible. A ship could have set course along the straight line from Andøya via Bear Island to Half Moon Island. But Haugen had to take the wind into account. It had the aircraft at its mercy and could blow them way off course. However, Haugen could read the strength and direction of the wind from a network of lines and mysterious signs that criss-crossed and dotted the chart. He knew when it shifted and could counteract its blows by feeding new courses to the pilot.

Haugen was by far the busiest man on board. He took readings from a bank of instruments that measured the plane's position and drift, but most of all he was a breathing computer that spewed out figures from take-off to landing.

Haugen and Lieutenant Strande were great friends and never let a chance for a friendly quarrel go by. Both were expert at coming up with ironic hints about each other's professional or personal traits. Strande claimed, among other things, that he had once sought Haugen's advice about two watches—one that lost a second every hour and one that had stopped completely.

"Use the one that's stopped," Haugen had said. "That

way you'll at least have the right time twice a day. As
for the other one, it'll only be right once every ten
years."

By the time they approached Bear Island, Haugen had
developed a gnawing hunger. He was a late riser and had,
as usual, skipped breakfast. "Anybody want a slice of
bread?" he asked over the intercom.

"Yes, please," said Strande. "Much obliged. With
cheese."

"Now listen here. You know I don't have time to make
sandwiches," retorted Haugen indignantly. "I just thought
maybe somebody could fix *me* one, while they were at it."

"Oh . . . well, I'm not *that* hungry."

The flight engineer was dozing in his chair in the back
of the plane. Since most of his job was done on the
ground, he was usually the one to fix the food. He fumbled
drowsily for the mike.

"You fellows think this is some kind of a restaurant?"
he complained. "We're not even halfway there, yet. I'll
fix lunch an hour before we land."

"By then I'll be starved to death," Haugen insisted in a
faint voice. "That's not till"—they heard him page
through the log—"12.29."

"One minute to twelve-thirty," Strande noted. "Science
has spoken. Darned impressive to be able to think that
precisely without having hair to scratch in."

After a lot of arguing back and forth Haugen finally got
his sandwich. "Chef's special for grouchy stomachs,"
announced the flight engineer. A big dill pickle crowned
the concoction.

Strande asked after a short silence: "How was it?"

29

"The bread was fine," replied Haugen. "But it sure was tired sausage."

They cruised at five thousand feet with the sun beaming from a clear sky. Beneath them the scattered clouds grew gradually denser. Ahead, though off their course, a high formation of cumulus towered like a deformed mountain range. The summits were white as chalk in the bright sunlight.

Bear Island was hidden under the cloud layer and could only be seen on the radar scope.

Captain Henriksen sat relaxed, humming his everlasting tune. The automatic pilot kept the plane on course and at the correct altitude. The pedals and controls moved by themselves; none of the pilots touched them. But both Henriksen and Strande were more alert than it seemed. They scanned the instruments at regular intervals and were ready to take over at a moment's notice if the need arose.

As Haugen's lines and symbols closed in on Hopen Island and the radar operator announced that he had that landmark on the scope, Henriksen was given a new course that carried them due north.

"In eight minutes it'll be time to slip down through the clouds," said Haugen. "The mountains of Edge Island should at least be within sight then."

And he was right. They levelled off under the ceiling and could just make out the mountains like a blue mirage against the drab sky. The sea was fairly calm with long, flat swells and no sign of white caps.

But the first thing they caught sight of as they neared Half Moon Island was the white froth of waves breaking against the rocky shore. The island itself was almost one with the sea and was in reality little more than a big flat rock, lifting its barren and desolate face above the waves. It rose in gentle slopes from all sides. There were no shrubs or trees on the island, only boulders, rock falls and patches of yellowed grass and moss around small lakes. A wide belt of sand along the shore was specked with driftwood and innumerable stones ground smooth by the crashing waves.

Captain Henriksen studied the island as they swept by it. The breakers told him from which direction the wind and current came. Only a few of the small coves were sheltered and had quiet, almost mirror-smooth water. There was no snow yet. The bare, rock-faced shore glistened with moisture as if it had just rained, but farther north the steep slopes of Edge Island were covered with new-fallen snow halfway down to the shoreline. The rocky wall was capped by a glacier that stretched across the upper plateau as far as the eye could see.

The trapper's hut was located on the north side of Half Moon Island, perhaps a hundred yards from the sound that separated it from Edge Island. A wisp of smoke rose from the chimney.

Henriksen noticed that the wind was blowing almost at right angles to the waves. He banked out over the sound and descended for a dummy run before attempting a landing. As they skimmed the surface he turned the aircraft into the wind, and drifted half sideways, parallel with the rolling waves. The drift was stronger than he had expected.

But it didn't seem too bad. He took the aircraft to five

hundred feet again and alerted the crew. "Keep your belts tight, boys. Might be in for a jolt or two."

They descended on a long, gentle glidepath. Strande let out the flaps in stages each time Henriksen gave a short order. The surface rose quickly towards them as the plane lost speed.

"Stand by," warned Henriksen without shifting his gaze. "Get the flaps up and reverse the propellers the very minute I pull out of the wind and set her down."

"Sure," said Strande.

The engines were at half-throttle. The air speed indicator had passed ninety knots and was dropping towards eighty-five. The drone of the engines lessened as Henriksen gradually reduced power, and the whoosh of air against the fuselage took over. They swept low above the waves, nose up into the wind and the right wing dipped slightly.

All of a sudden, when a long swell came rolling towards them, Captain Henriksen swung out of the wind and flicked the throttles all the way back. The heavy seaplane smacked against the water. The keel cut into the waves, and all other sounds were drowned out in a violent hammering under the hull. It sounded as if the fuselage were ploughing through a field.

"Flaps up! Reverse props!"

Strande was ready. The levers were in place before the words were pronounced. Simultaneously, Captain Henriksen gave full throttle and the engines roared in response. The propellers jammed the air in front of them and whipped up the water into white foam that was torn loose from the surface and cascaded over the hurtling aircraft. The next moment the bow dug into a new wave. Masses of green water coursed across the windscreen and washed away. Henriksen clutched the stick in its rear position and kicked maximum rudder to keep the nose from ploughing under.

The aircraft had lost momentum. The water drained off the windscreen. The broad hull settled into the water and seesawed rhythmically as the wing floats rose and fell with the swells.

"Why haven't you guys applied for a submarine skipper's licence?" asked Haugen over the intercom.

They turned towards shore and taxied slowly in the direction of a small inlet that looked as if it would provide shelter from the waves.

"Look!" Strande exclaimed as they got closer. He pointed to a small peninsula inside the cove. "We should be able to tie her up there. The water's smooth as a whistle and the prop blades will clear that half-submerged rock with plenty to spare."

"Yeah—if the water's deep enough." Henriksen hesitated. He took off his headphones and turned to the navigator. "How's the tide?" he asked.

Haugen thumbed quickly through the flight almanac, ran his finger down a column of figures, and answered: "It's coming in."

"Good. We'll try it," said Henriksen.

They kept an eye on the primitive hut, hoping the trapper would be well enough to meet them at the shoreline. But the door remained shut. There wasn't a sign of the lonely hunter.

"Seems like the red carpet won't be rolled out today," remarked Strande. "We'd better take a stretcher ashore."

33

The flight engineer had entered the cockpit. He stood silently between the pilots with his eyes fixed on the shore.

"Be ready to open the door as soon as we're in calm water," Henriksen told him. "Grab hold of the rock with the grappling hook and hang on. Send Sparks ashore with fenders."

"O.K."

The hut disappeared from view as they glided into smoother water.

Strande had opened the side window and kneeled on the seat. He kept a sharp lookout at the bottom, which was easily visible through the crystal-clear water.

"Plenty deep," he said. "Sandy bottom with small round pebbles. No sweat. Keep coming."

Henriksen let down the wheels. They steadied the aircraft and would take the brunt of the shock if they ran aground. As they drew closer to the point he feathered the props and let the plane ride out the last of its momentum.

Some minutes later the Albatross was well secured. The rock they had tied up to was almost on a level with the door. They didn't need a landing plank; just one long step and they were ashore.

"Are we coming with you to the cabin?" asked Strande as he and Henriksen checked the fenders and mooring ropes.

"Yeah. The plane will be all right here, and we'd better bring as much as possible in one haul if we're going to get off again before dark. You have a pencil and piece of paper?"

"Sure."

"Good. You'll be responsible for making a list and

estimating the weight of whatever we take along. How much can we manage?"

"Can't remember. Haugen's got it written down somewhere. We can at least take more than usual since we unloaded all the sonar buoys before we left."

"Fine. We'll most likely be loaded to the gills. Good thing we didn't bring along more than was absolutely necessary."

No one suspected that this was precisely what they *had* done.

Lost

It gave Torgeir quite a shock when the Albatross landed on water. At first he couldn't understand what all the noise under the hull came from. He had expected the usual cushioned thump as the wheels met the runway and, alarmed by the surprising sound, he grasped for support at the underside of the bunk. Strangely enough, both Terje and Lise remained calm. They weren't prepared for either this or that, and took everything as it came.

Later, when the slapping of waves against the fuselage left no doubt as to what had happened, Torgeir tried to reason out why they hadn't used the airfield at Sola. The runway could be closed for repairs; that was one possibility. Another could be trouble with the landing gear. For all he knew there might be still other reasons, things he couldn't understand, and with that he put his mind at ease. They were probably not so far from the airfield that they couldn't walk there. Everything would be all right if they could just get out of the aircraft without being seen.

Torgeir waited impatiently for the crew to disembark. The hours spent under the bunk had been long ones. Terje and Lise had managed best, having slept most of the time, while he himself had been too keyed up to even think about sleeping. Mainly he was afraid, but he was also in a way proud. For once in his life he had done something that not everyone would have dared—something that people would talk about and maybe even put in the papers.

The twins started whispering to each other after the engines were shut down, but Torgeir put a finger to his lips to hush them. They lay perfectly still while the crew left the plane. Not until the voices had melted into a single murmur in the distance did Torgeir roll out from under the bunk. He stood up, a little stiff and sore, and tiptoed to the door.

It seemed to be a day full of surprises. He had expected to see a harbour with piers and houses. Instead he saw a desolate landscape with almost no sign of life. Not a house. Not even a tree. No people. Only rocks and moss and grass.

From geography class he had formed a mental picture of what the countryside around Sola would look like. But what he saw didn't match too well with what he had imagined. To be sure it *was* fairly flat. That much fit. But the farms, fields and sheep pastures he had read about were nowhere to be seen. They might be hidden behind the stony hills that blocked the view. So was the airfield, probably. And the town of Stavanger.

The twins came up behind him.

"Aren't we going?" Lise said. "Good grief, I've got to go." She shifted from foot to foot and her face had a hectic flush.

"Go ahead," said Torgeir. "I'll be with you in a minute."

He folded the blankets and put them back where they belonged. No other traces of their being aboard remained. He jumped out of the aircraft and headed ashore.

They walked up the slope that rose gently from the water towards what at first seemed to be a meadow, but turned out to be a fairly large lake. As they got closer they could see it was very shallow, with clear water and big stones on the bottom. Torgeir headed off to the right to get around it. From there the rise continued towards a low ridge with scattered crags and boulders.

It was amazingly quiet. At one point they heard voices, a shout and an answer. But they couldn't tell where the sounds came from.

For the most part they walked along smooth, even rock, just occasionally crossing grass-covered hollows and small glens. The grass was yellow and coarse. Dry moss grew in cracks in the rock bed. Behind them, on the other side of the f ord, a wall of mountains rose straight out of the water. They, too, looked barren.

The air was chilly, but they were dressed well, and grew warmer after walking for a while. They took off their scarves and mittens and zipped open their jackets.

"My stomach's growling," said Terje. "I'll pass out if I don't get something to eat soon." He closed his eyes and tottered along as if the worst were about to happen.

"Good grief, yes. I'm positively hollow inside," complained Lise. "Won't we come to a road soon?"

"Yes, soon," Terje assured them. He pointed ahead. "Beyond that rise. We'll get lots to eat when we find Dad."

"I could eat ten slices of bread," Lise said.

"Twelve," said Terje. It was his opinion that all figures, regardless of what they concerned, had to be higher for a boy than for a girl.

The slope proved to be longer than it had looked from below. The view was always shut off by low ridges and hillocks behind which they constantly found a small depression and another slope leading to another ridge. Terje and Lise began to straggle behind, and Torgeir's constant encouragement didn't seem to help. Finally, he gave up, and picked out a place where they could wait while he found the best way to go.

The twins rested on top of a rise and passed the time by throwing stones down the slope. Terje found flat pieces of slate that soared easily through the air. Lise was less talented. She used her whole body when throwing, and seemed to concentrate more on thrusting her bottom backwards than on flinging her arm forwards. No amount of good advice from Terje could get her to improve her style.

"Pooh!" she remarked. "I'm just throwing bigger stones than you."

Terje didn't bother to contradict her. He knew all too well that when Lise wanted to she could talk rings around him. While he had to pause for breath between words, Lise could produce a steady stream of sounds regardless of whether air was going in or out.

Therefore, Terje contented himself with a silent demonstration. He found a big piece of slate and sent it soaring in a long, flat arc that carried it far down the slope.

But when he turned around, Lise was squatting with her back to him, looking for pebbles. She hadn't even seen it.

In the meantime Torgeir had almost reached the crest of a hill that at last looked as if it tapered off to lower ground. He had jogged up the gentle rises and was out of breath and sweating. A sense of anxiety lurked within him and grew stronger the more he saw of the barren and desolate landscape. Perhaps they were further from Sola than he had thought.

Still, he refused to believe that anything had gone wrong until he finally stood at the top of the hill and saw water surrounding him on three sides. Only straight ahead did the land continue, at least as far as he could see. But the view in that direction was closed off by more rises and crests.

No houses. No roads.

The airport, the farms, fields and sheep pastures, everything he had expected to see, had to be behind the seemingly endless slope. But could that be possible?

He turned and looked back at the mountains across the fjord. Their massive flanks fell almost straight down into the water. That, for sure, wasn't the way he had pictured the surroundings at Sola. No, the airfield and the farms and fields had to be somewhere on the side of the fjord where he stood.

Or—could it be that this wasn't Sola at all?

The thought made him shudder. Had the aircraft made a

stop along the way? Maybe a *short* stop? Would they take off again? Soon?

He felt a wave of discomfort that he couldn't quite explain because he didn't actually *believe* what he was thinking. Everything seemed to indicate that the crew had left for the airport. Everyone had gone ashore. At least one or two of them would certainly have stayed aboard if they were to be ready to take off again soon. But why should they have landed at all in such an isolated place if there weren't a road that led to people—and probably a car to take them there?

Still, the airfield could be a long way off. That much he understood now. The aircrew might have had few sheltered coves to choose from, and had perhaps used the only one in the vicinity where the aircraft could be tied up safely.

Torgeir decided to go back to the twins. If he were to go any further, he would have to take them with him. But most likely the best idea was to return to the plane and look for the road the crew had taken. If the worst came to the worst and they couldn't find any road, they could spend the night in the aircraft.

It would certainly be dark before long.

He glanced up at the low clouds moving slowly across the sky. Had it grown darker already?

In his thoughts he visualized a night out in the open air. Terje and Lise would be terrified. He, too, for that matter. It would be pitch dark. And cold. Maybe rain. They would be hungry. Tired. With no opportunity to sleep . . .

They had considered themselves lucky when they

41

managed to slip out of the aircraft unnoticed. Now it suddenly seemed to be their only possible haven.

He turned abruptly and ran down the slope. His rubber boots were heavy and the ground uneven. He stumbled and fell, scraped his hands, bled, dried himself on his jacket and ran on.

His chest heaved. The noise of his breathing and the rush of air, whistling past his ears, prevented him from hearing the aircraft engines start. Not until the deep vibrations in the air had reached a steady rumble did he freeze in his tracks and listen, his mouth wide open. Fear crept up his spine like a cold chill.

Suddenly he was off again, with feverish urgency, staggering and unsteady among the sharp stones that lay scattered on the ground.

Terje and Lise came running to meet him when he appeared, but he brushed past them.

"Come on!" he shouted, but didn't take time to turn and see if they had understood him. He had only one clear thought—to stop the aircraft and escape the dreadful fate of being left alone so far from people.

The Albatross came into view behind the crags when he had almost reached the shallow lake. It was taxi-ing at half speed out across the fjord, trailing a wake of wind-whipped foam.

Torgeir stopped so abruptly that his feet slipped on the rock and he tumbled over. His knee landed with a thud against a blunt stone. Jumping to one foot, he limped around in a circle and struggled to suppress mounting sobs, then he was gripped by a fit of coughing that filled his eyes with tears and clogged his nose. He leaned against a large boulder and tried to breathe slowly to get rid of the rough feeling in his throat. It didn't work. He was too short of breath and had to gulp for air. New waves of coughing racked his slender shoulders.

When the worst was finally over, he climbed on top of the boulder, took off his jacket and waved it frantically in the air.

"Stop!" he cried. "Stop! Stop!"

It was all like a nightmare. Only for a short moment did a ray of hope strike him, when the plane paused momentarily and lay tossing in the waves. But then the throbbing roar came at him again, at double strength. The one engine revved up while the other continued to idle. The seaplane spun around in a tight circle as always when the engines were being tested before take-off from the sea. After a couple of rounds the roar died down and rose again as the other motor was cut in at full throttle. The propeller whipped a cloud of spray from the surface. The wake drew a frothing ring in the sea.

"Wait! Wait!" screamed Torgeir. He pressed his voice to the utmost. But he could just as well have whispered. No one could have heard him above the roaring engines.

Had anyone in the aircraft looked back, he might have seen Torgeir as a barely distinguishable dot against the stony, grey background. But all on board were too busy to give a thought to the naked Arctic island. The sound of monotone voices, electronic crackles and clicking switches mingled with the hum of the idling engines. The sick trapper lay strapped in the bunk and appeared to be asleep.

Captain Henriksen shoved the throttles forwards. The

wide bulk of the Albatross ploughed clumsily through the swells. But as it picked up speed, the aircraft lifted gracefully higher and higher on the surface until the wake was only a thin white line. The line was cut. KKG released the water and climbed heavily towards the gleam of light along the southern horizon.

Not one of the crew threw as much as a glance back at Half Moon Island.

The Cabin

It took a while before the twins trudged down to where Torgeir sat waiting. In the meantime he had dried away the sweat and tears from his flushed face, and tried to hide his concern by working intensely at a splinter he had gnawed loose from his ragged thumbnail.

"What's all the rush?" asked Terje. Both he and Lise were sulky and irritable. Neither of them had the slightest suspicion that anything serious had happened. They had hardly noticed the Albatross as it climbed skywards. The sight of an airborne plane was much too commonplace to attract their attention. What really bothered them was that they were tired and hungry and didn't want to walk any further—especially not if they were to end up where they started anyway, panting and sweating.

Torgeir had an unusual feeling. He sensed a raging anger welling up within him. No doubt the twins would be less cocky if he told them about the mess they were in. They had no idea that they had baited him into stowing away on the aircraft. Nor did they know that there probably weren't people for miles around, that they had no place to stay and nothing to eat. Pretty soon it would be dark. And it wasn't even certain that they were anywhere near Sola.

But he didn't dare tell them. Not yet. The difficulties would only pile up if they became frightened. They would give up all hope and burst into tears.

Torgeir was on the verge of tears himself. It was almost impossible to hold back the sobs. But he had to stick it out. He was fourteen, the twins only eight. What chance did they have if he gave up?

Maybe—maybe it wasn't as bad as he feared. They might happen upon a road if only he could get the twins to go a bit further.

Terje and Lise stood quite still, studying his face and waiting for him to say or do something. They held each other's hand.

Torgeir stared for a moment in the direction in which he had seen the aircraft disappear. It had vanished into low clouds while still climbing and might have changed course later on. He had heard the drone of the engines die out after a while. But whether it was because the aircraft had passed out of hearing range, or because it had landed somewhere, he didn't know.

He hauled himself to his feet and explained wearily: "We went the wrong way. We'll have to try again."

Unwillingly the twins followed him back to the shore. They passed the cove where the aircraft had been moored and without knowing it headed off along the same path the crew had followed earlier. At the top of a small rise they caught sight of the trapper's cabin.

"A house! A house!" Torgeir screamed ecstatically. The twins came up from behind and looked at him in amazement. They found his enthusiasm for an old tumbledown shack completely incomprehensible. In their opinion a store or a bus stop would have been a better find.

The twins should be given their due. The cabin was a sorry sight. It was grey, sagging and wretched, built from a jumble of timbers and planks of different lengths—a rough patchwork with slanting corners and small, shuttered windows. Tar paper was fastened to the roof and to one of the walls with pieces of moulding and scrap lumber.

Some yards away was a shed that leaned to one side as if it were about to collapse. Most likely it was a woodshed or a privy, or both. Behind it, on a wooden stand a half yard or so off the ground, lay a row of tin drums—perhaps of gasoline or kerosine, or something of the sort.

"No one's lived here in a hundred years," said Terje.

Torgeir didn't answer. His attention was fixed on the thin stovepipe that stuck up through the roof of the cabin. He studied it closely to make sure his eyes weren't playing tricks on him. But they couldn't be. A thin wisp of smoke rose from the pipe and was whirled away in the wind.

"Someone's at home!" he cried excitedly. "Come on!"

The joy was short-lived. They found the cabin door nailed shut with a solid board, a simple lock which showed that the owner didn't intend to return soon. Even the window shutters were firmly tacked to the wall.

"But someone's just been . . ." Torgeir stopped in midsentence. Had those who lived here moved? Had the aircraft come here to pick them up? Was there perhaps no road after all?

He shivered. But not because it was cold.

Lise's hand groped for his. "It's beginning to get dark," she whimpered.

"Yes." He had been aware of it for some time.

"We'll have to stay here tonight," he said. His voice was thick.

"Here?" the twins asked in unison.

He nodded and swallowed. "It's too far to walk to the airfield today. We don't even know the way."

"But then—we'll starve to death," protested Terje, not knowing how close he might be to the truth.

"We may find some food in here," said Torgeir.

He knocked on the door with the knuckle of his index finger, producing a strangely weak sound on the heavy boards. It was something like knocking on a brick wall.

He tried with his fist.

"Is anybody ho-ome?" he called. His voice cracked. He cleared his throat and tried again. No answer. Not that he had expected one.

He made a half-hearted attempt to loosen the board, but it wouldn't budge by so much as a hair. The nails were thick and substantial. He looked around for something to use as a lever, found a broken shovel beside the cabin wall and worked it in under one end of the board. The nails let out a godforsaken screech as he heaved on the makeshift crowbar. But they gave way. He threw the spade aside and yanked off the board.

The door opened a little when he tugged on the handle. But something on the inside resisted, something that could be forced, but constantly pulled in the opposite direction. Involuntarily he let go of the handle and jumped back a step.

"What is it?" whispered Terje. He whispered so loudly that he might as well have shouted.

"It's . . . it's . . . it's just—stuck," Torgeir stammered.

Behind him he heard the twins breathing. Except for the distant rumbling of the waves surging against the rocky shore, all was very quiet. Dusk had closed in.

When he had gathered his thoughts again and felt convinced that no living soul could possibly be hiding inside a boarded-up cabin, Torgeir braced his knee against the doorframe and hauled on the latch with both hands. The opening widened. He worked his knee into the crack and held the door ajar while he peeked inside. The shaft of light from the narrow slit fell on a stone that hung suspended in the air. It dangled from the end of a rope looped over one of the rafters.

Was it a trap?

Torgeir was tempted to give up. The house seemed so dismal and uninviting. But he had no choice.

He shoved his shoulder into the crack and forced the door wider open. The stone moved. It seemed to rise a bit higher, swaying slightly. The door hinges groaned and the rope creaked. But when he relaxed his hold and let the door slip back a little, the stone began to fall, and he let out a sigh of relief. Putting two and two together he understood that the rope and stone were used as a primitive lock. No doubt the other end of the line was fastened to the door so that the weight of the stone would keep it closed.

His fear subsided somewhat. He concentrated all his strength on squeezing through the door opening, and he got inside. It was pitch dark. He fumbled for the rope, found the knot and pulled at a loose end. The stone crashed to the floor.

In his bewilderment Torgeir stumbled backwards against the door and tumbled out of the cabin. Terje and Lise got the impression that he had been *thrown* out. They turned tail and fled with a terrified screech.

"Wait!" screamed Torgeir. He staggered to his feet and ran after them.

But they hadn't got far. Both of them had tripped in the murky evening light and lay flat on their faces, howling in chorus.

"Stop it!" Torgeir shouted, trying to drown out their screams. His nerves were on edge. "There's nothing to be afraid of. Come on—we can go inside."

"No. No. I don't dare." Lise got to her feet and backed away.

"Come now," coaxed Torgeir, calling on his last reserves of patience. He took them by the hand and pulled them along with him. Lise resisted. Her hair dropped down in front of her eyes, and her face was streaked with dirt where she had rubbed away the tears. Terje wasn't much braver, but at least he didn't struggle against Torgeir's grip.

They halted in the doorway and peered in. As their eyes grew accustomed to the dark, they could make out a sparsely furnished, unpainted room. There was a table and two or three straight-backed, wooden chairs. Alongside one of the walls were two bunks, complete with blankets. In one corner stood a small, pot-bellied stove.

The air drifting through the doorway was discernibly warmer than that outside. The smoke from the stovepipe had not been an illusion. Someone had been in the cabin quite recently.

Torgeir entered the room. There was a lamp on the table, filled with kerosine. A box of matches lay beside it. He lit the wick and set the glass in place.

A change came over the room. It seemed much larger, and the cheerlessness that had seemed to lurk in the dark corners almost vanished. In the innermost corner, Torgeir discovered another door. He opened it and looked out into a small annex tacked onto the cabin. It was the kitchen. In the faint light he could barely make out the outlines of a stove and a counter, a cupboard and another bunk. This was where they might find some food, if there was any.

The twins had at last mustered up enough courage to cross the threshold and they tiptoed into the room, their bodies poised as if ready to whirl and run out again at a moment's notice. Torgeir closed the outer door behind them and bolted it from the inside with a bar that fit through two angle irons. He filled the stove with wood and put a match to it. At least they had plenty of firewood.

There was a large crate packed with grey logs. The stove was lukewarm and a smoky smell still rose from the ashes.

Gradually the twins' normal voices returned. They stopped whispering and their wary glances into the corners of the room became less and less frequent.

"Might as well check the kitchen and see if there's any food," said Torgeir. His tone of voice was optimistic, but his hand trembled as he lifted the lamp and carried it into the annex. Terje and Lise followed at his heels, keeping within the circle of light cast by the lantern.

There were only cups and saucepans in the cupboard.

Under the counter were three drawers. Torgeir opened the top one and found it filled with knives, forks and spoons.

He tensed to the point of pain. Lise and Terje pressed closer. They were hungry and wanted supper, but their concern stopped there. Only Torgeir understood that something far more important might be at stake.

He held his breath as he opened the middle drawer.

"Hurrah!" shouted Lise.

Their heads bumped together as they all leaned over to look.

The drawer was filled to the brim with food. It literally bulged with cans and plastic bags. In some of the transparent bags they recognized sugar, flour, oatmeal and many other staples. The cans had different shapes and sizes, but Torgeir didn't take time to find out what was in each of them. He slammed the drawer shut and opened the bottom one. It contained more food, mostly cans—meatballs, fishballs, stew and tomato soup.

Terje fished out a can and read aloud from the label: "Spaghetti and meatballs."

"I want this one," he announced. Then he glanced questioningly at Torgeir. "That is, if we can take it."

"We'll borrow it," said Torgeir. He gestured invitingly with his hands and nodded towards Lise. "How about you? Take your pick."

She chose the same as Terje.

There was firewood in the kitchen as well. The logs were chopped into pieces of just the right size for the stove. Torgeir had no difficulty getting a good fire going. He found a soot-covered saucepan on the floor beside the stove, opened two cans of spaghetti and emptied the contents into the pan. Shortly afterwards, when steam began to rise from the bubbling sauce, a delicious aroma wafted through the cabin.

They set the table in the main room. The pot-bellied stove was giving off plenty of heat. The fire crackled merrily and spots of reflected light fluttered restlessly across the floor.

They took off their outer garments and sat down to eat. All things considered, the situation looked a whole lot brighter. The twins regained their good spirits, thinking it exciting to be runaways. After the edge was taken off their hunger, they became talkative and burst readily into fits of laughter.

Only once did the mood again become depressed and cheerless. Terje happened to remark: "Now they're searching for us. But they surely think we're on Andøya. What if Dad flies home to help in the search—without knowing he just has to *walk* here to find us."

"Yeah. Golly—" said Lise, showing her deep concern by forcing half of her wrist into her mouth.

But Torgeir said nothing. He looked blankly at Terje. Then he rose abruptly to put another log on the fire.

A Search in Vain

Shortly before the grey dawn dispelled the darkness of the night, an Albatross passed Risöyhavn and closed in on the airport at Andøya. Pale rays of moonlight broke through the scattered clouds and rippled across the sea. Otherwise the surface was black as wet asphalt.

Captain Dag Solheim dimmed the cockpit lighting and squinted towards the bleak halo of light on the northern point of the island. He could not yet make out the runway beacons.

The trip from Sola had been as long as a bad dream. The Albatross seemed to inch along even though he pushed it to the limit. From the moment he had received word that his children were missing, his thoughts had been centred on getting to Andøya as fast as possible to help search for them. Every half hour he had asked over the radio if they had been found, but the answer was equally depressing each time. Their disappearance seemed quite inconceivable. He couldn't imagine Torgeir and the twins going far from home without telling their mother what they were up to. It was no less than a mystery how they could have got lost.

Dag cut a bulky figure in the cockpit. His shoulders were a little rounded because he often had to duck to avoid doorways and other low obstacles. He had a squarely chiselled face which could seem tough and stern, but his gaze was friendly and inviting.

He sat in silence and stared into the darkness. Inwardly, he ached with impatience, but his large hands rested calmly on the controls.

The lights on the island began to appear like pinpricks in a black curtain. Some of them arranged themselves in two parallel rows. The runway was right ahead of them.

The co-pilot established contact with the flight controller and received clearance to land. They passed the shore and descended northwards, parallel with the main runway. The apron in front of hangar B was floodlit. Dag could see a large group of people huddled together by the hangar door. He was apparently expected. Inger Marie, his wife, would be among them. She, too, had no doubt had a sleepless night.

He banked out over the sea and turned onto the glide-path. The runway lights glistened in the windscreen like strings of beads. At the far end lay the apron, a glowing square in the dark. Almost silently, with the wind whooshing along the fuselage, they drifted down through the night and crossed the runway threshold. The lights came at them in pairs and flashed by. Rubber screeched against concrete, and the weight of the aircraft shifted almost imperceptibly onto the wheels.

As he taxied up to the platform, Dag got a glimpse of Inger Marie standing beside the tall, lean station commander, Colonel Holm. She seemed to be clutching her fur coat tightly around her as if she were freezing. He hurried through the cockpit check and scrambled out. Seconds later she was in his arms. She shook like a leaf. Her finely moulded face was flushed and puffy and her unkempt hair fell loosely over the collar of her coat.

"We haven't found them," she sobbed.

He couldn't think of anything better than to whisper: "There, there now. Don't worry. We'll find them as soon as it's light. They can't be far away."

"But where can they be, then?" she whimpered. "Hundreds of men have been searching all night."

He repeated half to himself, half to her that they would be found somewhere or other as soon as it was light. Then he gently withdrew from her arms and greeted the station commander, who was waiting a few yards away.

Colonel Holm echoed Dag's opinion. "They can't have got far," he said. "To be honest I think they've simply gone into hiding. They'll come out as soon as they're hungry enough."

"But why in the world would they—?" Dag began.

Colonel Holm interrupted him. "You haven't heard the whole story," he said. "It started quite harmlessly this morning with a common fistfight between Torgeir and a schoolmate, but thanks to Terje it ended rather dramatically. He waded into the fight with a hockey stick and clubbed the other boy so hard that he had to be taken to the sick bay suffering from a head cut and concussion. My guess is that your kids were terrified of the consequences. They ran away and probably don't dare show their faces."

Dag was both shocked and relieved at the same time. "What was the boy's name?"

"Arne Halvorsen."

Dag nodded. "I know who he is," he said. "How is he?"

"Just fine. He'll be good as new in a couple of days. But he needs rest because of the concussion."

"I've been to visit him," said Inger Marie. "He's a bit of a roughneck and has taken it all in his stride. It looked fairly bad when they brought him in, though."

"As soon as we've located the kids, I'll stop by the sick bay," said Dag. "What do we do after daybreak?" He turned to the colonel again.

"I've called a meeting in half an hour to organize the search. You can come along and hear for yourself." ·

"Fine, thanks."

"Want a ride in my car? I'm ready to leave as soon as you are."

Inger Marie took Dag's arm.

"You're going to have breakfast first, aren't you?" she said. "I can drive you to the base afterwards." Like many people she regarded food as a universal cure when things went awry.

"Later," said Dag. "You fix breakfast, dear. Set the table for five. We'll eat when we're all together again."

He laid his arm around her shoulders, followed her to the car and saw her well off before joining Colonel Holm.

During the ride to the base at Skarstein the colonel explained what had been done so far. A couple of aircraft had been sent up, but the flights were literally a shot in the dark and had led to nothing. By first light they would try again. The ground search, however, had been going on all night. Several hundred anti-aircraft men, shouting and waving flashlights, had combed the marshes and nearby woods. The county sheriff had called everyone in the vicinity who had a telephone, asking them to check their sheds and boathouses—and to notify their neighbours. In the morning the sheriff would take inventory of the row-boats in the area to see if any were missing.

The colonel stroked his cheek. He sent Dag a quick glance. "Do you think they could have pinched a boat? Are they that kind of kids?"

"Not the oldest. I wouldn't put anything past his brother, but when they're all three together Torgeir's the one who's in charge."

"That's a comfort." The Colonel smiled. "We can probably assume they haven't set off to sea then. We'll soon find them in good shape."

They stopped outside Wing Headquarters, entered the building and walked along a corridor to a door marked "Operations Room". Underneath the sign some practical joker had tacked a drawing of white-robed nurses and a surgeon preparing to operate on a patient with a huge carving knife.

The operations room was a long, narrow affair, lit by a string of glaring neon lights. Behind a long desk at one end of the room were the operations officer and a sergeant hard at work. The sergeant tended a telephone exchange and had direct contact with a number of other bases and air-fields. There were maps and display boards all over the walls. On the inside of the door hung a poster with the acid comment: *If you have nothing to do, don't do it here.*

Three or four of the other officers had already arrived. Two of them, the chief of operations and the squadron commander, were old friends of Dag. They shook his hand gravely. There was an awkward silence in the room until Bjørn Henriksen turned up and aimed a friendly jab at Dag's chest.

"Hi, Dag," he murmured in his deep voice. "Chin up. Before long it'll be light so's we can fetch those kids home, smack their bottoms, give them breakfast and call it a day."

"Sure." Dag nodded.

The door swung open and shut without pause as groups of smoking and chattering men filled the room. Most of them were dressed in green field uniforms and had their trousers tucked into high rubber boots. Some had walkie-talkies slung over their shoulders.

The groups broke up when Colonel Holm mounted the stand beside the wall map of the airfield and surrounding area. For a moment the room resounded to the scraping of chairs as everyone found a seat. Then there was quiet.

"It's almost dawn," said the colonel when all faces were turned towards him. "From now on we'll make use of everything we can to complete this operation. First let me get an idea of what we have to work with. How many planes?"

"Three." The chief of maintenance removed a bulky briar pipe from his mouth. "One of them is scheduled for an operational mission, but the other two are available. In three or four hours I expect to have another one ready.

Plus the aircraft from 330 Squadron, of course, if Captain Solheim is supposed to fly."

Many pairs of eyes glanced fleetingly at Dag.

"We can see about that later," Colonel Holm said. He shifted his gaze to the anti-aircraft battalion commander. "How many men have we got?"

"A hundred and twenty who have had six hours' sleep. They're getting ready now and can move out in half an hour."

"Vehicles?"

The transport officer exchanged a quick glance with the chief of maintenance who waved a go-ahead with his pipestem.

"We can spare six, Colonel, three Volkswagen buses, two Volvo station wagons and a flatbed truck. They're due to assemble at the staging area in fifteen minutes."

Colonel Holm stared thoughtfully at the tips of his shoes. His mouth was hard set and a pair of muscles moved imperceptibly under the skin of his lean cheeks. Dag's presence distracted him. He had to choose his words with care.

"Well . . ." He looked up and waited for those who had filled the pause by counting nails in the ceiling to lower their eyes again.

"Let's sum up what's happened so far." He checked off the points on his fingers. "First, the fight that started the ball rolling. Then the kids fled. They were scared and wanted to get away. The next thing we know is that they talked to Flight Sergeant Myrmo outside Hangar C. Since then no one has seen them.

"Their mother searched alone for many hours. It was

late afternoon before I was contacted, and we had a search underway within the hour. But by then it was practically dark."

Holm picked up a pointer, traced a line on the wall map and continued: "We've covered this area so thoroughly that we can hardly have missed them—provided they want to be found. But we can't be sure about that. We'll have to assume they might be hiding and are too afraid to come out. Consequently, we'll search the entire area again in daylight.

"Here is my plan:

"Chief of Operations keeps two aircraft in the air as long as the search is on. They will both concentrate on the woods and mountains.

"Battalion Commander makes use of all cars except the two station wagons and assigns patrols to scattered sectors within the search area.

"Chief of Administration places six non-coms at the sheriff's disposal. They'll drive around in the station wagons and get people to look in their barns, sheds and boathouses.

"We've been promised a helicopter from Bodö or Bardufoss. Once they're in the air I want the Albatrosses to hold an altitude of at least a thousand feet.

"That's all for the time being, I think. Patrols with mobile radio sets will be contacted if there are any changes. If the operation is called off I'll let an Albatross overfly the area dipping its wings. Any questions?"

One of the younger artillery officers raised his hand. "What about first-aid equipment, sir. If it's needed?"

"The ambulance will stand by at the hospital. Send an order to the nearest radio post with a message."

"Colonel?"

"Yes." Holm nodded to Dag.

"Is it all right if I go along in the helicopter as a look-out?"

"Yes—that's just fine. If the kids have headed for the mountains, they're quite sure to follow familiar paths. And you know best where they've been before."

Colonel Holm shot a glance at the window. It was almost light outside, and time to get going. Dag, and many of the others, had gripped the arms of their chairs and were ready to rise at the first sign of adjournment.

"O.K., men," said Holm. "Let's get moving."

For a minute there was a confused bustle in the operations room. Buzzing low voices mixed with the tramping and shuffling of heavy boots. But the stream of men drifted quickly out of the door. The Colonel left last, stooping slightly. He had been up all night.

Dag made a brief stop at the canteen. He gulped a quick meal before the chauffeur picked him up and drove him to the airfield where the helicopter had arrived.

Half an hour later, when he strapped himself into his seat beside the pilot, the sun had barely risen over the crest of the mountains east of Andsfjord. The low glare made them flip down the sun visors on their helmets. The pilot prepared to take off. He opened the throttle and the idling rotor increased speed. The whine of the jet turbine was gradually drowned in the clatter of the rotor blades. The fuselage rocked lightly on the undercarriage.

On the other side of the ramp Captain Henriksen sat in the cockpit of an Albatross going through his checklist. He paused momentarily and watched the helicopter.

"I have a feeling that neither planes nor helicopters will win the day," he said to Lieutenant Strande who was looking over his shoulder. "The kids are either hiding, in which case they'll come out when they're hungry enough, or, or—God knows what's become of them."

He tugged thoughtfully at his chin while the helicopter lifted and hung suspended a few feet off the ground, as if reluctant to go through with an act so obviously in defiance of the laws of nature. When it then whooshed skywards as if gravity didn't exist, he shook his head almost in disbelief and returned his gaze to his own instrument panel.

"Like the caterpillar said as a butterfly flitted by," Henriksen mumbled.

"What did it say?" invited Strande.

"You'll never get *me* up in one of those things."

Life in the Wilderness

It was morning.

Torgeir opened his eyes and looked dumbfounded around the half-darkened room. It took several seconds before he remembered that he was lying in the primitive kitchen of the cabin. A few rays of sunlight filtered into the room through cracks in the weathered shutters.

The place seemed even more wretched than it had by lamplight the night before. The walls and ceiling were made of trimmed and untrimmed boards nailed haphazardly together. Some were broad, others narrow. Some had once been painted, though the last traces of colour were nearly gone. A bulky and discoloured sheet of tin had been nailed to the wall behind the rusty stove, and the stovepipe disappeared through a sooted hole in the ceiling.

Sometime, somewhere, Torgeir and a few of his friends had collected crates and hammered together a clubhouse.

It had more or less resembled the cabin. Only the size was really different.

Not a sound came from outside. He heard nothing but the even breathing of Terje and Lise in the other room.

The time was ten o'clock. Cold air prickled his arm as he stuck it out from under the covers to look at his wristwatch. He wished he could pull the covers over his head and pretend it was all a nightmare. But there was nothing unreal about his hunger.

When his growling stomach finally out-argued his reluctance, he bolted onto the icy floor and hastily pulled on his clothes. Then, cautiously, he tiptoed into the room where Terje and Lise apparently were still asleep. But Lise's voice stopped him before he reached the outer door.

"Where are you going, Torgeir?"

"Out to take down the shutters," he answered.

Terje's bed squeaked. He got up on one elbow and peered sleepily at Torgeir.

"But aren't we going to Dad right away?"

"Sure we are." Lise jumped out of bed and grabbed for her socks. "Sure. You don't need to take down the shutters."

"Oh well—anyhow we have to eat breakfast first," Torgeir said. "The airport might be far away, you know. Just get dressed. I'll be back in a minute."

He stood for a few seconds and chewed at the nail on his middle finger, then opened the door. Light cascaded in. There wasn't a cloud in the sky. The sun shone on the snow-clad mountains across the fjord making them seem

66

much closer than they had the day before. The air was cooler, and there was white frost on the ground where the sun hadn't reached.

Outside the cabin it was so quiet he could hear his own breath. His footsteps on the stony ground resounded against the cabin walls as he crossed the yard to the small, tottering shed. When he opened the door to peek in, the squeaking of the rusty hinges reminded him of a scream and gave him goose pimples. The floor inside was stacked with sawed and quartered firewood. A sled and two pairs of old-fashioned, worn-out skis were leaning against a wall. In one corner there was a privy. Long rows of huge nails had been hammered halfway into the walls like a series of hooks, but nothing was hung on them.

Under an extension of the roof outside lay a pile of logs and boards, all of them grey and weathered. The rack of gasoline drums stood some yards away, sheltered by a low crag.

Torgeir wondered what the drums could contain. He tried to rock one of them, but couldn't budge it. He sniffed around the taphole without smelling anything, then noticed that one of the caps had been replaced with a spout. A clear fluid ran out when he opened it, and the smell was unmistakable. It reminded him of trips in the mountains when they had cooked coffee on a portable stove. The drums were filled with kerosine.

But why did the owners of the cabin need so many of them? Six drums in all. Did the stock have to last a long time? Was it so far to the nearest store?

Only questions ran through Torgeir's mind. No answers.

67

He found the broken spade he had used to pry open the door and went to work on the shutters. It was an easy job. The shutters were fastened with smaller nails than the door. They gave way easily and tumbled to the ground. Terje and Lise appeared inside the windows and made faces at him.

"Did it get light in there?" he shouted.

"Yes," they replied in chorus.

After this intelligent exchange he went back inside.

They needed water to make breakfast. Torgeir estimated that it was only some hundred yards to the nearest end of the shallow lake they had seen the day before. The twins offered to go.

"Too heavy," protested Torgeir.

"A bucket of water?" Terje was visibly offended. "I can carry it with one finger," he assured his brother.

"Without spilling any? Have you tried?"

"Yeah, well—tried? 'Course I have."

Torgeir had his doubts. But he had to rustle up some food and get a fire going in the kitchen stove. It would save time if he had help.

"Don't fill it up, then," he said. "Half full is enough. And carry it between you."

"Oh, there's no harm in having lots of water," expounded Terje and darted out the door with Lise at his heels.

Torgeir went to the kitchen and opened the middle drawer in the counter. He had planned to make pancakes if he could remember how to mix the batter. But all he knew about cooking was what he had learned in domestic-science class at school. It had been easy then, but he regretted now that they hadn't been required to memorize recipes. The only ingredients he was sure of were flour and sugar. The biggest bag in the drawer contained flour. There was a flourlike substance in another bag that crackled like snow when he squeezed it. He hadn't any idea what it could be.

Anyhow, as he rummaged through the contents of the drawer he came upon a number of pleasant surprises. One of them was a can of powered milk. He read the label carefully and learned that it was possible to make milk out of water. It was quite amazing, but the instructions said so clearly. The same was true of the text on another can containing powdered eggs. It plainly claimed that he could make eggs out of powder. What would they think of next? What use was there for hens then? To lay shells to put the powder in?

He laughed at his own train of thought. It cheered him to find that he could still come up with a joke.

Having searched at length, but in vain, for butter, he brought out a green bottle filled with some sort of oil that he understood could be used instead—at least in the frying pan. He decided on pancakes and set about getting a fire going in the oven. Meanwhile he pondered over how long the food supply would last. One week, two maybe. It depended on how many pancakes he could make with the flour, and that was a riddle he couldn't answer.

He went to meet the twins and found them behind the cabin staggering along with a quarter bucket of water between them.

"It splashed something awful," said Lise and laughed. "Terje's boot is full of water. When I helped it only got worse. It sloshed over all the time. Splish-splash, splish-splash—first on me, then on Terje."

She almost choked with laughter.

Terje looked at her sourly. Then he too bubbled over. "Splish-splash," he howled and slapped his knee. "Ha, ha—he, he."

Torgeir carried the bucket inside. The twins took off their boots and put their wet socks to dry on a chair by the stove. While waiting for the pancakes, they sat in bed with one leg under the covers and played hearts with a ragged deck of cards they had found in the kitchen cabinet.

When breakfast was ready, Torgeir pulled the table over to the bed. The pancakes went down in no time flat. They smelled and tasted as they were supposed to, and were at least as good as those they were used to at home.

It suited Torgeir fine that the twins' boots and socks were wet. That gave him a chance to go out alone and get his bearings. He asked the twins to stay put till he had found the best way to the airfield.

"Pretty far off, I believe," said Terje. "Haven't heard a plane all day. Not one. Not many, anyway."

"Me neither," Lise said.

"May be a crosswind on the runway," suggested Torgeir.

They accepted the professional-sounding explanation without reflecting on the fact that there wasn't more than a slight trace of a breeze outside. Torgeir put on his windbreaker, paused a few seconds with his hand on the doorlatch, and left.

He chose a new and easier route than the one they had

followed the day before. It was almost noon and he had the sun straight ahead. That meant he was heading south. The fjord and the mountains were behind him, to the north.

The sun didn't provide much warmth and it puzzled him that it was rather low in the sky. Obviously it should reach higher above the horizon in southern Norway than it did at Andøya. But there had been a lot of rain the past weeks and he hadn't seen much of the sun. He probably remembered wrong.

By keeping well to the left of their earlier path he headed almost directly towards the small rises that had blocked his view at the point where he had turned back. He walked briskly but didn't run—not until he had almost reached the top. Then the excitement became over-whelming and he broke into a spurt that brought him panting to the highest point.

What he saw made him freeze in his tracks. He stood wide-eyed and stared, as the full horror of the situation sank in. They weren't at Sola at all.

They were on an island!

The sea stretched in front of him, grey and foaming, as far as the eye could see. Nothing more.

The terrain was the same as he had seen before. Sloping rocks, small outcroppings, boulders, grass and moss. Not a single house. Nothing to indicate that there were people on the island.

He stood still for a long time. His eyes were dry, but his features had tightened into an expression that made the face seem older. He scanned the island in vain for signs of life. Everything, except the sea, seemed silent and im-movable.

The shape of the island resembled that of a half moon and Torgeir estimated the size at a three hours' march in length and half as much in width. The sound between the island and the mainland was fairly narrow. He could clearly see rock falls on the steep mountainsides, but no trees on that side, either. The mountains were all about the same height and were rather flat on top. From crest to shore ran deep clefts where snow had been trapped in the shadows.

The cabin was the only thing that indicated there could be people nearby. And it probably wasn't used very often. Whoever would want to live on a rocky island where nothing but yellow grass or lichen could grow?

If people lived here at all, it could only be on the mainland, behind the high mountains.

How quiet it was.

Torgeir captured the silence with all his senses. No birds chirped, no streams gurgled. The wind swept noiselessly over the treeless, stony island.

He headed back to the cabin. Tears began to trickle down his cheeks making cold tracks in the skin. It was no use brushing them away. New ones followed.

"Two times sixteen is thirty-two," he thought and tried to concentrate on the problem. He searched for a more demanding one. "Nine times—nine times a third," he hesitated a moment, ". . . is three."

As he approached the cabin he began to limp, first on his right foot, then the left. He grimaced and whimpered as he opened the door and tottered across the threshold.

"I've sprained my ankle," he moaned. "I can't put any weight on it. We'll have to stay here another night."

The Storm

The one night became many. Torgeir still limped and the trip to Sola had to be postponed from one day to the next.

One late evening, after the twins had fallen asleep, Torgeir lay back in his bed, anxious for some rest. But many thoughts churned through his mind and sleep came grudgingly.

Mostly he was concerned about their food supply—how much remained, how far the leftovers would reach, and how best to make them last as long as possible. Before extinguishing the lamp he had browsed through a cookbook that Terje had found under his bed together with some newspapers and magazines. The book was old and yellowed and many pages were missing. Still, Torgeir found it exciting reading. Both pancakes and porridge could be made in other ways than he had been doing, and there were other recipes he wanted to try as well.

He pulled the covers up to his nose and decided to count to a hundred to see if he would fall asleep before getting that far. But it didn't work. He had only reached fifty when he thought he heard voices whispering outside the cabin wall. Instantly he was wide awake. He pulled the covers from his face and lifted his head from the pillow. At first he heard nothing. Then the sound returned, stronger this time, a kind of mumbling that rose and fell and then disappeared.

Torgeir felt a strange tingling in his scalp, as if his hair were standing on end. He breathed through his mouth so as not to make a sound. Carefully he raised himself to one elbow and fumbled in the dark for a matchbox. But in the next instant he forgot all about the matches, suddenly aware of a new and different sound.

It came from far away, a strange vibrating tone in the air, a hushed roar like a choir of deep bass voices. Gradually the chorus became more resonant, and higher tones were added as well as a rattling, whistling sound that constantly increased in strength.

Swish—s-h-h-h—s-h-h-h.

Again he heard the whispering sound outside the cabin wall. But this time he could tell it wasn't voices. It was a gust of wind streaking by. After such a long period without the slightest breeze, it seemed almost unreal.

The distant humming became steadily stronger as if it were drawing nearer. The sound slammed down from the sky, surging and receding like voices screaming in agony.

Then all at once a giant hand grabbed hold of the cabin. The storm broke loose with explosive force—like a landslide, an avalanche, a dam that suddenly burst. The floor and walls trembled. The woodwork screeched and groaned. Streaming winds howled alongside the cabin, tugging and tearing at loose parts. And through the tumult of whining, hissing, squeaking and clattering sounds came a two-voiced howl from the main room.

Torgeir jumped out of bed and groped around for matches. A chilly draught swept through the cabin and made him shiver in his light underwear.

Terje's thin voice barely reached him: "Torgeir!"

"Yes." He could hear that his answer wasn't loud enough, and he shuffled across the floor, arms stretched out in front of him, until he got hold of the doorframe.

"Yes," he repeated.

"It's blowing something awful."

"Yes, I can hear it."

"The walls are shaking. The whole cabin will come down."

"Don't be silly. Of course it can stand a storm." Torgeir wasn't nearly as convinced as he tried to sound.

"It's not a storm. It's a hurricane!" Terje shouted.

"It is a hur-ri-cane!" screamed Lise. She intoned the word with all the fright it brought to mind.

The fear in their voices made Torgeir grimace in the dark. They had said what he was afraid even to think. This couldn't be an ordinary storm. There was something wild and destructive about it that he had never before experienced. Could it be powerful enough to crush the cabin?

He chewed frantically on the nail of his little finger, mindless of the stabbing pains it caused. A splinter came loose and pulled some of the nail's roots with it.

With the regularity of a metronome something crashed against the wall outside and made a sound like a cracked bell. Clunk—quiet. Clunk—quiet. The noise might have been the same if a ram had tried to raze the cabin with determined butts. Torgeir thought first it was a kerosine drum, and expected it to come crashing through the wall at any moment. When he remembered having brought a garbage can down from the shed he breathed a sigh of relief. The empty can could do no harm.

"Get some light on!" Terje shouted.

Lise supported him. "Get some light on," she echoed.

"Wait a minute!" Torgeir groped his way back into the kitchen, found a box of matches and lit the lamp. His shadow danced like a giant phantom across the walls and ceiling as he carried it into the other room.

The twins sat up in bed and squinted at the light with frightened eyes. Their faces were ashen in the faint glare.

"*Is* it a hurricane, Torgeir?" whispered Lise.

The word had an ominous ring to it. Actually, none of them knew what a hurricane really was. They pictured vaguely some powerful wind, stronger than a storm, that mostly blew on the oceans, or in America. They had heard or read somewhere that it crushed everything in its path, overturned houses and sank ships.

"It's just a storm," said Torgeir.

Occasionally a flash of light streaked across the pitch-dark windowpanes. There was lightning, but they could hear no thunder. It was either too far away, or was drowned in the roar of the gale.

The garbage can stopped hammering. It was suddenly

torn loose and began to roll. They listened as it scraped and jangled against the stony ground until it disappeared out of hearing.

Torgeir stood in the middle of the room in his underwear, his teeth chattering. He ran into the kitchen after his clothes and dressed quickly. The shivering abated a little though the draught rushed cold as ice through the room. Trying to get a fire going in the stove would certainly be hopeless. There was a hollow rumble in the pipe and a puff of soot would every now and then drift through the vent and settle like fine powder on the floor.

"Lie down, now," Torgeir said. "Try to get some sleep."

He regretted the words the moment they were spoken. He had no desire at all to sit up awake by himself. But the twins had no intention of going to sleep.

"I don't dare sleep," whimpered Lise, huddling deeper into the covers. "What'll we do if the house goes to pieces?"

"Don't think about it. The cabin will hold up. It'll soon be over."

"I think it's getting worse," Terje said meekly. His usual spunk had blown away with the wind. "Do you believe . . . ?"

His question was left hanging in the air. At the same moment the door burst open and slammed against the outer wall with a thunderous crash. The cabin sagged as the raging storm swept in. Their ears popped from the mounting pressure. The lamp went out. A casserole rattled across the kitchen floor, and the chair that Terje had hung his clothes on toppled over.

The twins dived under the covers with a scream.

Torgeir's thoughts stood still. He felt a strange emptiness in his head. Perplexed he searched through his pockets for matches, but let them drop the moment he found them. It would be pure stupidity to try to light the lamp again.

His clothes flapped madly and the noises surrounding him were like the shouting and tramping of an angry mob.

He crouched and battled his way clumsily to the door. For a long time he just stood there, clinging to the doorframe. Then he heaved himself out.

The storm hit him with brutal force. It wrenched his feet aside and toppled him to the ground. A powerful gust swept him along the outer wall like a helpless bundle. He screamed like mad, but no one could hear him. His hands flailed wildly for something to hold onto.

Digging his fingers into the ground he at last managed to halt the wild tumble. Dazed and stricken with fear he began to crawl back. It was like bucking the swift currents of a swollen river. The howling squalls pounded into him, locking his shoulders and arms in a vice, seeking to tear him along with them. The pressure of the wind filled his mouth and nostrils and threatened to suffocate him. He gulped for air. His face seemed to swell, his temples throbbed and white dots danced against the back of his eyes.

With each move he had to search for a new handhold. He clawed at rocks and tufts of grass, hung on for all he was worth, ripping and tearing his fingertips until he sobbed with pain.

The noise was literally earsplitting. Penetrating sounds and discords blended in chaotic confusion with only the thunderous crash of waves against the shore recurring regularly. Even in the dark he could make out the frothing white caps. They stretched skywards like veiled ghosts and crumbled into nothingness. The wind carried the seaspray ashore. He could taste the salt on his lips. His soaked and sticky hair was plastered against his forehead.

Torgeir was unaware of how long the uneven fight lasted. He moaned and panted, screamed with fear when a hand or foot slipped, dug into the ground and crawled on. Exhausted and aching in every bone and muscle he finally reached the doorway and clung to the threshold. The door pounded like a sledgehammer against the wall. It couldn't be long before it was ripped loose from its hinges.

Dead tired as he was, Torgeir would have given anything to be able to crawl across the threshold and find a sheltered place where he could lie down and let everything take its inevitable course. But he was aware that the cabin couldn't stand up against the furious squalls as long as they had free play through the open door. Something would sooner or later give way. The windows would shatter, a board would come loose, then another, and another—until everything collapsed. Only one thing could save them. The door had to be shut.

And there was no one, no one in the world, who could help him. He had to do it himself.

But how? His weak muscles were no match for the compact power of the wind blasts.

Still, he struggled to his feet, took hold of the latch on

the careening door and hauled with all his might. It was useless. One moment the door was plastered flat against the wall, the next it would be sucked away and become trapped between the thrust of the wind and the backwash on the leeward side. It stood there quivering until a new gust slammed it once again into the wall.

Torgeir was pulled and dragged along with it. A few times he banged his head so hard against the door panel that sparks flashed before his eyes. In a way he was lucky. Had he managed to get the door past the balance point it might have slammed shut and crushed him mercilessly against the frame.

He gave up and sought shelter inside the doorway. His face was contorted with pain and exertion. Despair swept over him as he stood there in the darkness, not knowing which way to turn.

Then something brushed across his shoulder. It was the rope that still hung looped over the roof beam, the primitive lock that they had neither used nor taken down. Now he could also distinguish the drooping coil that was suspended between the beam and the solid hook on the door.

An idea struck him, a faint possibility. Could he manage to close the door by pulling on the rope? He groped around in the dark for the rope end, caught hold of it, pulled in the slack, then hung on, waiting for the door to swing away from the wall. When that happened the rope came sliding across the roof beam. He fell to his knees and held tight. But the next moment the door was flung against the wall again and the rope jerked brutally from his hands.

It was no use. He was too weak. Nothing seemed to help against such a wild force. He might as well submit to hopelessness and crawl into the dark to hide. It would be good to be able to cry.

He crawled across the floor, trying to reach the corner where the oven stood. Along the way he collided with a chair. Then he heard, for the first time since the door had sprung open, a sign of life from the twins. It was a desperate cry from Lise: "Torgeir! Torge-i-r!"

He didn't answer.

He lay there irresolutely, clinging to the chair. Then he set off again—creeping backwards in the direction he had come from with the chair dragging along behind him. He shoved it under the roof beam, close enough to the wall to be sheltered slightly from the wind. But it was still a tricky task to get up on the chair in the darkness and the heavy draught from the doorway. It took several tries before he got hold of the beam with one hand and the rope with the other. For a long while he was totally absorbed in what he was doing. Laboriously he wrapped the rope twice around the roof beam and waited for the wind to slacken. When the door swung out he pulled in the slack with both hands, twisted the coils around the beam and let his entire weight sag against the rope end. The jerk came, but this time the rope bit into the wood. The door stayed put. The stretch of rope between the beam and the hook vibrated like the taut string of a violin.

Soon the rope slackened again, less but more quickly. He managed only to haul in an inch or two before the rope once more was taut. But he waited patiently for the smallest twitch of the door. He fought grimly to hold on to the little he had won. And to win a little more. A little more....

His strength was almost expended and his arms ached when something happened—so suddenly that Torgeir tumbled in fright from the chair. A fierce gust caught the outside of the door and slammed it shut with a crash like the report of a heavy gun. It was suddenly almost quiet. The roar of the storm seemed distant, as if it had died away.

Torgeir stood up as cautiously as an old man. He groped his way to the door and laid the crossbar in place. It went from one side of the door to the other through large iron squares under the latch and on the frame. No wind could break it.

"Torgeir!" Another cry came out of the darkness. He stood trembling with his forehead resting against the doorframe. His body was wilted. His hands and knees quivered.

"Yes," he answered, but couldn't even hear himself. The sudden stillness was not as deep as he had thought.

"Yes, I'm here," he said, louder.

He dragged himself across the room and found the lamp and the matches on the table. The lamp's chimney was shattered. But there were extra chimneys in the kitchen cabinet. He replaced the broken one and lit the lamp.

"I was so frightened," Lise whispered. "I was afraid you couldn't get the door shut."

He sat down on the edge of her bed without looking at either of them.

Terje stared at him. "How *did* you do it, Torgeir?"

"It blew shut," he said.

He said nothing about how tired he was. He didn't show them his bleeding hands. In amazement he thought that only one thing counted.

It was something that had to be done.

And he had done it.

Winter

In the morning hours the storm began to die down. None of the children had slept a wink. Hour after hour they had sat quietly with their eyes fixed on the flickering flame of the lamp—the twins with the covers up to their chins, Torgeir bundled up in a wool blanket on a chair.

Never before had they experienced such a storm. The autumn and winter gales at Andøya had sometimes been harsh enough, but at home they could always look forward to crawling into bed while the howling winds raged outside. There were always other, comforting sounds mixed in with the noise of the storm—a car driving by, the ticking of an alarm clock, the radio playing in the living-room, or Mum and Dad's voices. Here there was no comfort at all; every nuance of sound was filled with dreadful savagery.

Terje was the first to become his old self again. Bit by bit as the storm subsided he lifted his head higher, his eyes regained their sparkle, and he resumed his usual chatter.

"I think it was an American storm," he said. "It probably came clear across the Atlantic."

When no one answered, he added with most of his cocksure tone of voice intact: "But it had likely died down a lot along the way. In America they yank skyscrapers right out of the ground and send them flying."

Lise gasped, but Torgeir wasn't much impressed.

"Not skyscrapers," he said. "Occasionally a house or two can be destroyed."

"All houses in America are skyscrapers," Terje answered.

"Oh, no—only in the biggest cities. New York and some others. Elsewhere they have houses just like ours."

In Terje's eyes this was a gross underestimation of America, but he let it pass. "They're called Anna and Bertha—the storms, that is," he announced, a bit subdued.

"Pooh," said Lise. "They haven't other names than hurricane and the like."

"Yes, they do, you know." This time Torgeir supported Terje. "Hurricanes are named in alphabetical order. The first each year is called something beginning with A, the next one B, and so on."

"Why are they given girls' names?" Lise wondered.

"Because they howl and scream so much," suggested Terje.

As soon as the rumble in the stovepipe subsided and Torgeir had made sure that the draught was flowing in the right direction, he stuffed some logs into the stove and got a fire going. The cold was bitter and the room a sorry sight with furniture overturned and clothes and other things strewn everywhere. But Torgeir wasn't as particular as usual. He straightened up the worst of the mess and let it go at that.

On occasions the fading wind threatened to return. Boards creaked as gusts whooshed around the corners, and the stovepipe rumbled again. But nothing more came of it.

At regular intervals breakers exploded against the shore. They frothed and gurgled as they rushed back to the sea, were quiet a moment, then thundered in for a new attack.

They had oatmeal for breakfast. It was a bit watery, more like soup than cereal. But it tasted all right and took the edge off their hunger. Torgeir had followed the recipe in the cookbook regarding everything but the amount of water to use.

While they were seated at the table the night began to lift. Torgeir had just helped himself to seconds when he suddenly dropped his spoon, spattering oatmeal across the table. With a bound he started from his chair and ran to the window. He pressed his nose against the pane and shielded his eyes from the reflection of the lamp. Something white drifted past the windowpane.

"It's snowing!" he shouted.

In the grey light of dawn it was like looking into a huge white cavity. Fifty yards away everything was hidden behind a dense veil. The air was filled with whirling white particles. The ground lay hidden under a sea of sculpted drifts. In a few short hours winter had set in.

The twins came shuffling barefooted across the ice-cold

floor. They looked out, gasped and ran back to their bunks.

"Doesn't matter," said Terje. "We've got skis. Two pairs anyway. As soon as your foot is—is all—healed . . ."

He stammered and fell silent.

Torgeir thought to himself: "Have I slipped up? Have I forgotten to limp?"

He couldn't remember, but made sure the limp was obvious when he returned to the table. He finished his meal hurriedly and cleared the table.

The snow continued to fall. It fell silently, for the wind had slackened altogether. The breakers were also subsiding and made just a whispering murmur they no longer noticed. Instead they pricked their ears to catch a new sound from far away. At first they feared the storm was returning. But the noise wasn't quite the same. It drew slowly nearer, a deep grinding rumble, broken now and then by sharp reports. They hadn't the slightest idea what it could be.

"But—but Torgeir, what do you *think* it is?" harped Lise.

He had gradually got the knack of telling white lies. All the same, he couldn't think of any this time.

Now and then they went to the doorway and peered out, trying to locate the origin of the noise. But not before the day began to wane, bringing a break in the snowfall, did they discover what it was. Terje, as usual, had the sharpest eyes. It was he who suddenly darted out through the door and pointed. "Look—what on earth is that? The fjord is all white. It's—it's packed with—ice!"

The others only gasped.

The ice came drifting into the sound from the east. In the far distance it had already created a white bridge to the mainland, a moving compact mass that shifted and crammed and squeezed its way between the shores on either side. It seemed alive, constantly assuming new forms. Large sheets rose on end, ground against one another, overlapped, cracked and shattered. The crushing, grating noise was no longer a puzzle.

But Torgeir wondered silently: "Where *are* we? Where in the world are we?"

Lise shook like a leaf.

"So many strange things are happening, Torgeir," she sobbed. "Oh, gosh. Why do so many strange things happen here?"

Torgeir had no answer. He was stupefied. But he began to suspect the worst.

"Come on," he said as loudly and flippantly as he could. "Let's go inside. The ice can't do us any harm."

Terje went first and held the door. "How far is it to Sola?" he asked as Torgeir passed by. "Is there this much ice at Sola?"

"You know as well as I do that they have to use ice-breakers even in the Oslofjord sometimes," Torgeir fended.

"Yeah, but—"

"Oh—stop it! You'll jabber a hole in my head with all your questions," shouted Torgeir abruptly, tramping on the floor. His mouth twitched at the corners. He fled into the kitchen and started rattling around with something on the stove.

A while later he came into the other room again. He

stuffed another log in the stove and sank heavily into a chair. The twins sat silently and helplessly on their beds.

"I don't know where we are," said Torgeir.

They just stared blankly at him as if unable to comprehend what he had said.

"There's nothing to be afraid of," he told them comfortingly, trying to keep his voice from quavering. "They're sure to find us. Meanwhile we have shelter and food and firewood."

"You don't know where we are!" Terje said. It was beginning to dawn on him. "Aren't we at Sola?"

"No."

"But—"

"We must be somewhere in northern Norway. Finnmark maybe. Before long someone will come looking for us."

"How will they know where to look? Who are they? Why aren't they here already?"

"Dad—and many others. First they'll search around home. When they can't find us, they'll come here."

"But how far do you think we'd have to go to find people?"

"No one lives here. We're on an island."

"An—island?" Lise couldn't hold back the tears. She tried in vain to suppress her sobs.

"Shut up," whimpered Terje, struggling not to be affected. He swallowed several times before he was able to go on: "What'd the plane come here for? When nobody lives here?"

"Someone *was* here when we came. The plane picked them up."

"How come?"

"Don't know. Maybe somebody was sick."

They fell silent and listened to the growing tumult from the ice-packed sound. Torgeir crossed to the window and gazed towards the white mountains. There were no roads there. No houses, either. Still—it had to be somewhere at the foot of those peaks that the people in this part of the country lived.

"We have to make a bonfire," he said, half to himself. "I'll go out and build a fire. If we light it after dark, they'll see it a long way off and will come and get us."

He went to get his cap and mittens. Lise followed him with her eyes.

"Why—is your ankle well again, Torgeir?" she asked wide-eyed. "You're not limping any more."

A Close Shave

Overnight the entire sound became jammed with ice. Large floes had been piled up on land along the shore, and new masses of drifting ice pressed on from behind. Flakes and floes, blocks and small icebergs fought for room in the narrow channel. Cracks appeared and closed again. The swells rolling underneath made the frozen surface pitch. The grinding of ice against ice hung in the air like an uninterrupted roll of thunder.

Some days later all became quiet. The sea hardened. Drifting snowflakes found their way into the cracks and smoothed the rough edges. Finally the sea stretched in all directions like an endless icy field. The island was land-locked.

But hollow rumbles and sharp reports revealed that there was still movement in the frozen landscape. An eternally shifting pattern of cracks and leads drew lines in the rugged expanse. Frost steamed from them. The temperature had fallen. It was biting cold.

One day the twins decided to try out the skis. By packing the snow on a hill just outside the cabin, they made a track that could carry them all the way to the shore. But the skis sat loosely on their rubber boots. They had trouble steering, and were forced to fall on purpose to keep from whizzing out onto the ice.

Torgeir was pleased that they had found something to occupy them while they were outside during the disappearing hours of light. The days were quickly growing shorter, and it was difficult to fill the long evenings with suitable pastimes. The twins became bored and thought too much about food, of which they had lately been given less and less.

Torgeir himself had plenty to do while it was light. He sawed and chopped wood, tapped kerosine from the drum and shovelled a path from the door to the outhouse. The bonfire they had built also had to be cleared of snow, and he added to it constantly. They had given up lighting it in the evenings. Three nights they had tried, but there was no sign that anyone had paid any attention to it. Now he merely kept it ready and was prepared to light it in a hurry if they should hear an aircraft coming.

Twilight set in before Torgeir had finished his chores. He was tapping kerosine from the drum when he decided it was time to get the twins inside. There was still an eerie glimmer of light on the chalk-white mountains across the sound. The passing day ruled a narrow swath of sky over the horizon, while stars appeared like pinpricks in the velvet canopy above. A prelude to the evening's northern lights had already begun. Pale shadows flickered fleetingly across the snow.

He turned off the spout and groped in his pocket for the cap to the kerosine can.

Then he heard a frightened shout.

"Torgeir! Help! Help!"

He dropped the cap and ran. There was terror in Lise's voice. He saw her coming from the shore, stumbling through the deep snow. She stopped abruptly when she caught sight of him, turned and pointed emphatically.

"Terje!" she sobbed. "Terje fell through! Into the water! In the water!"

"Where, Lise? Where? Where is he?"

She broke into a run, screaming unintelligible words. He followed hard on her heels and caught sight of a cap and two mittens sticking up behind an ice floe not far from land. From that second Torgeir stopped reasoning. Without a moment's thought he leaped in long bounds across the floe, threw himself down flat and half slid, half crawled until he crashed through about a yard from Terje. A sheet of ice had broken in two, and the gap was filled with a thick, soggy slush. It pulled him down like quicksand. The water enveloped him with an ice-cold shock.

He struggled feverishly to get his arms out of the slush. It was like swimming in paste. He gasped from fright and lack of air. With peculiar frog-like movements he fought his way towards Terje, and managed to get hold of his jacket. During a single frantic second he got a glimpse of the drenched and deathly pale face.

"Come on, Terje!" he screamed, half choked. "Kick! Kick! Come on!"

But Terje wasn't much help. He moved slowly as if benumbed with cold. He got hold of Torgeir's neck, hung on and pulled them both down.

The slush closed in over Torgeir. Salt water and bits of ice filled his mouth. He kicked desperately with his feet in the open layer below the slush. The icy water had soaked through his clothes and covered his skin like stinging, frosty armour. His muscles began to stiffen.

When he got his head above water again, he had shoved Terje away. But the first few seconds he had more than enough difficulties of his own. He splashed around like a madman, spitting blindly. His breath burst in moaning spasms from the tortured lungs. The need for air was so overpowering that he forgot all else.

Terje lay half submerged when he finally regained hold of him.

"Hang on!" he shouted without knowing what he really wanted him to do. He tugged at Terje with stiff, powerless arms, and got him up against the edge of the ice floe.

"Get a hold, Terje," he wheezed. "Claw your way up."

His lips were numb; the words were an almost incomprehensible babble. But Terje reacted a little. With clumsy, helpless movements he got his arms up on the ice, while Torgeir battled to lift him out of the water. During the wild struggle Torgeir went under for a second time. But he got a grasp around Terje's knees and shot to the surface with a powerful kick. The momentum had a decisive effect. Terje went over the edge, rolled over on his back, and lay there lifeless with his feet dangling in the water. The tip of one of his skis stuck out of the slush.

Torgeir was about to pass out from exhaustion. His chest ached unbearably, and streaks flashed before his eyes. He had used up all his strength. His muscles were completely numb. All at once he realized that the worst, the impossible, remained. He couldn't get himself out alone.

Terror gripped him as never before. He lost his hold and gulped another mouthful of slush and water.

"Li-ise!" he screamed.

And, as he lay panting for breath, using his last ounce of energy to stay above water, he saw Lise coming.

She was crawling on all fours, tears streaming down her face and shoulders shaking. But her eyes didn't leave him for a second. In front of her she shoved one of her skis.

A moment later he had hold of it. He kicked wildly with his feet, got his chest up on the floe, and twisted, sprawled and rolled onto solid ice.

Afterwards he lay perfectly still. His senses told him that he was unable to stand up. All the same he had to! Clumsily, and with painful slowness, he got to his knees, reached out for Terje, and dragged him along. He didn't look at Lise, didn't ask for help. Like a speechless animal he crawled towards land with the motionless bundle behind him.

Lise did what she could. She unstrapped Terje's skis, grabbed hold under his shoulders and struggled backwards up the slope. It was she, and not Torgeir, who got Terje into the house. The last half of the way Torgeir left everything to her, and tottered in front of them towards the cabin.

The warmth inside brought him to his senses. They

helped each other to get Terje undressed. Bits of ice tinkled across the floor. The buttons had to be torn loose. They got Terje to bed and wrapped him up in all the covers and blankets they had. He stared at them with glazed eyes and didn't answer when Lise spoke to him.

Torgeir pulled a chair over to the stove and tore off his own clothes. He was chilled to the marrow. His lips were almost white, his face a sallow grey. His teeth chattered. He couldn't get out a word.

But Lise guessed what he needed. She found him a towel and blanket. In time she became more and more active. She fussed over them both like a concerned mother hen and bustled around hanging frozen clothes to dry on chairs, nails in the wall or wherever she could find an available place.

Torgeir rubbed himself down until his skin began to tingle. But as blood began to flow again in the contracted veins, intolerable pains surged through his body. His nails throbbed as if about to fall off. He bundled the blanket around him, crouched down, and danced a strange tribal dance around the stove.

Terje tossed restlessly under the covers and wailed. The warmth brought frightening pains to his body as well. But Torgeir was relieved. Anything was better than the limp, lifeless body he had dumped into bed. The wailing showed that his brother was alive.

As the pain and shivering slowly subsided, Torgeir felt the reaction coming on. His eyelids grew heavy and he yearned to escape it all by settling into a deep sleep. At last he slumped into Lise's bed and in a matter of minutes was fast asleep.

96

The day was done.

Lise sat on a chair and stared straight ahead. When one of the boys breathed heavily or moaned or tossed in bed, she held her breath and squeezed her hands folded in her lap. She put an extra log on the fire when needed. The temperature in the room had risen. Pearls of sweat popped out on her upper lip.

Outside in the dark the wind whistled softly around the corners of the cabin. The windowpanes were black. But every once in a while a silver-white reflection shimmered in the glass.

The northern lights set the sky aflame, writing their fiery script amid the stars.

Hard Days

When Torgeir awoke he felt warm and rested. He lifted his head from the pillow and smiled at Lise, who sat up straight and beamed.

"Are you all right again?" she whispered.

"Not bad. How's Terje?"

"Sleeping. But he's so restless. Sometimes he moans and makes whining sounds in his sleep. Do you think he is dreaming?"

"Most likely. Must have got the scare of his life."

"Weren't you scared?"

"Sure. How about you?"

"Who, me?"

He raised himself to one elbow.

"It was you who saved us, Lise," he said.

"Pooh—" An embarrassed smile crossed her lips. "Your clothes are dry," she said to change the subject.

She handed him the underwear that had hung by the stove and become heated throughout. The warmth flowed delightfully through his body as he pulled on the garments.

"This week's laundry was free," he joked. "But next time I think I'll take the clothes off first."

He tiptoed over to Terje's bed and glanced at him worriedly. He was asleep. But he looked ill. He breathed in quick, wheezing gasps, and his face was grey and clammy. Only his cheeks had any colour—a hectic, flushed red.

Torgeir knew that there was a box filled with medicines of all kinds in the kitchen cabinet. He found it and studied the labels carefully. The only one that was familiar was aspirin. The word penicillin on a small brown jar of white tablets also seemed to ring a bell. In parentheses further down on the label was written *pneumonia*.

Torgeir took two aspirin tablets, then laid the box back in place for the time being. He put the tablets and a glass of water on the table to have handy when Terje awoke.

Lise got ready for bed. They hadn't eaten since breakfast, but none of them gave a thought to food. Torgeir's wristwatch showed about midnight. Luckily it had withstood the icy bath.

During the night Terje's condition worsened. One moment the perspiration poured from his burning body, the next he was gripped by a fit of cold shudders. At times he trembled so violently that the whole bed shook. The skin on his forehead and around his eyes was taut and white as a sheet.

Lise made breakfast when she got up in the morning.

99

She did her best to come up with something that resembled pancakes, but all the sugar was used up, and the result wasn't exactly a culinary masterpiece. If they had not been so famished, they might have had trouble getting it down. But they didn't leave a scrap, even if Terje refused to eat as much as a bite of his share. He would only drink water. Torgeir sprinkled some crushed aspirin in his glass from time to time, and Terje downed it as if he couldn't tell the difference.

Later in the day he was periodically overcome by a violent cough. Foam collected in the corners of his mouth and his burning face swelled up. Between attacks he either dozed or stared straight ahead with glassy eyes. His fingers twiddled restlessly with the covers.

In his feverish dreams, his mind was elsewhere, and he constantly called out for Mum and Dad. Otherwise he spoke incoherently, running the words together, so that neither Torgeir nor Lise could make any sense out of what he said.

Once, when Terje was seized by a particularly bad attack, Torgeir asked himself: "Could it be pneumonia?"

But he had thought out loud, and Lise whispered: "Is that dangerous?"

He couldn't bear any more white lies.

"Think so," he said. And a bit later: "But we've got medicine for it."

"Why don't you use it, then?"

"Don't know if I dare. Could be the wrong medicine."

"Well, yes . . . but. Maybe he'll get well."

It was tempting. Torgeir got out the jar and read the instructions—two tablets every four hours. He had to make a decision—one way or another. Reluctantly he dissolved two of the pills in water, and got Terje to drink it.

Again he spent the whole night beside the bed, following from hour to hour the effects of the medicine. He didn't dare sleep. Perhaps he dozed off a few times. His head would become heavy and sag against his chest. But then he would awake with a start and his eyes would dazedly scan the room for a point to fix on before they relaxed once more.

The lamp's wick was turned down low. In the corners of the room it was almost completely dark.

Some time before dawn, Terje received his fifth dose of penicillin. He broke out shortly afterwards in a streaming sweat and in an instant his pillow was soaked. Torgeir was terrified. He dashed to the kitchen for a towel and some water, wet the towel and dabbed Terje's face and hair with it. He turned the pillow, but very soon it was just as wet on the other side. In frustration he hurled the penicillin jar into the kitchen, and vowed never again to experiment with medicine. When Lise got up in the morning, he was almost as pale and haggard as Terje.

"I've prayed for someone to come find us," Lise said. "Won't Dad be here soon?"

"How should I . . ." began Torgeir. But he changed his mind.

"Maybe," he said more mildly. "They've searched so long now—at home. I think they'll come soon."

Lise sat with her elbows propped on her knees. Her knuckles pulled the skin back from her temples making tiny slits out of her eyes.

"But they can't land on ice?" she said, half as a statement, half as a question.

"No—but once they know where we are they'll come and get us with a helicopter."

It was beginning to get light. Torgeir flung open the door, and the draught swept into the room like a cold shower.

Dawn was still only a vague shimmer above the eastern horizon. Touches of red and lilac highlighted the scattered clouds. Fluffy banks of mist drifted with the gentle wind across the ice.

He stood a long while in the doorway, poised as if listening for something. Then he closed the door and sat down by the bed again. An hour later Terje opened his eyes and looked up.

"Morning," he said.

Torgeir gulped. He nodded, but couldn't get out an answer. Lise reacted more quickly. She came silently to the bed and smoothed out a fold in the covers. Terje shifted his gaze.

"Morning, Lise."

She was exultant: "Are you well?"

Her hands stroked the covers again and again.

The slightest trace of a smile came to his dry, cracked lips. "Almost," he said.

Suddenly Lise was full of life. She clapped her hands and literally pranced about. "Do you want some food?" she chirped.

He shook his head.

"Just water."

In a flash she was in the kitchen. Out she came a moment

later balancing a glass filled to the brim. Torgeir placed a hand behind Terje's neck and steadied his head while Lise held the glass to his lips. He drank every drop and lay back against the pillow.

"But you haven't eaten in almost three days," said Lise, disheartened, ever mindful of her household duties.

Again he smiled almost unnoticeably. His voice was groggy. "So tired," he mumbled. "When I wake up—I'll eat—a horse."

"But—but we don't have a horse." She laughed merrily. "You can have pancakes."

"M-m." He closed his eyes. In a moment he was fast asleep.

Torgeir stood up. He was stiff and sore. His shoulders slouched deeply as he shuffled into the kitchen. He crawled into bed with his clothes on and pulled the covers over him.

When Lise later heard sounds from the kitchen, she appeared in the doorway. Torgeir's shoulders were shaking with convulsive sobs.

"B-b-but why are you crying now?" she asked, overwhelmed with astonishment. "Now that he's almost well again?"

But her voice wasn't very steady, either. She stood with her lips pressed together in a peculiar way, like Mum when she was sewing and had her mouth full of pins.

Leavetaking

The moving van started up and swung out of the driveway at Merket. Dag and Inger Marie stood by the window in the empty house and watched as the van turned onto the highway and began the long trip to Sola. Everything they owned had been loaded into the truck. Shortly they would themselves climb into the red sedan that stood parked beneath the window and set out on the same journey.

Half-heartedly they took one last look around the apartment. Nothing had been left behind. There were light patches on the bare walls where pictures had been. When they had hung them there almost four years ago, they had been a happy family of five. The twins had just had their fourth birthday, and Torgeir, at ten, was in the fourth grade. Now the Andøya years were over. And they were leaving alone.

The search had been fruitless. They hadn't found the

smallest sign, the slightest clue as to the children's whereabouts, and everyone had finally given up. It was no use pretending there was any hope. The children had vanished without a trace. They must have perished in some inexplicable way.

Inger Marie had been the last to give up hope. But even she had been forced to face the facts. Now they were packed, and all their belongings, furniture, clothes—everything—were sent off. When they arrived at Sola, it would all be in place in the new apartment. But the most important thing of all would be missing. They would be leaving Andøya deprived of what they could least do without.

They had said good-bye to their friends the day before. Bjørn Henriksen had lingered to the very last. As Dag's best friend, he was almost as unhappy as they were.

But neither he, nor anyone, could be of any more help.

"Come, dear," said Dag. "There's nothing left to do here."

They walked through the empty rooms, took along the suitcases that stood in the hallway, and got into the car. Dag switched on the ignition and pulled out onto the main highway.

It was a cool, clear day. The sun stood low in the sky and tinted the newly fallen snow on the upper peaks with a golden glare. Thin sheets of ice had formed on the small ponds in the marshes.

They followed the highway south towards Risöyhavn. From there they would cut across Hinnöya Island to the new bridge at Tjeldsund. The road would then turn southwards again carrying them almost the entire length of the country to Sola. They had a long journey ahead of them. The fact that they weren't looking forward to it made it seem even longer.

When they had passed the intersection at the Kjölhaug moraine Inger Marie laid her hand on Dag's and asked him to stop.

"I want to take one last look," she said. "I'll never come back here again."

He pulled over to the side of the road and switched off the motor. Inger Marie rolled down the window and slowly scanned the marshes, mountains and the familiar houses in the Skarstein Valley.

"Do you think they drowned?" she asked impulsively.

There was a long silence.

Dag clenched his teeth. At last he said: "You've got to try to think of something else. You'll drive yourself crazy by constantly brooding over it."

"I've tried," said Inger Marie. "But I can't seem to get it out of my mind. You've got to give me time."

Dag took out a pack of cigarettes and they smoked for a while without speaking.

"No—I don't think so—that they drowned," said Dag as if she had just asked. "I've thought about it a good deal. No boats were missing. One of them might have fallen in from a wharf or slippery rock, but there were three of them, mind you. Lise couldn't swim, and Terje could barely keep his head above water. If Torgeir had fallen in, he could have saved himself. If one of the twins had slipped, Torgeir would have jumped in to help. But in any case one of them, at least one, would still have been ashore. *One* would have run for help."

Inger Marie said nothing for a while. She tossed the half-finished cigarette out the window. It fell with a sizzle onto the soggy ground by the roadside.

"But what in heaven's name could have happened?" she asked, burying her face for a moment in her hands. "You combed every square yard in the entire area. You had aircraft, dogs and even frogmen from the Navy to help you. The children can't just have disappeared into thin air."

Dag laid his hand on her arm.

"Are you still hoping?" he asked quietly.

"I don't know. I only know that I can't bear the uncertainty. I must find out what happened."

She cried now, silently. Tears trickled down her cheeks and collected on her chin in large drops that fell on her coat.

"No use brooding over it," Dag said. "Whatever happened, it's over now. If they suffered, at least they're not suffering any more. Not now."

She grasped at this straw for support. But it wasn't enough.

"Torgeir must have taken them away to protect Terje," she said. "It must have been terribly hard on him—when it turned out as it did. He took the responsibilities of an older brother so seriously."

Dag thought for a moment.

"Strange," he said. "I believe he spent more time with the twins than with kids his own age."

Inger Marie pressed her lips together and bowed her head. She toyed with her wet handkerchief.

"He didn't have many friends, you know. Not here at

Andøya. Something happened when we came here from Gardermoen, I think. He must have missed his old friends so much that he had trouble making new ones. And you know how it is—someone's always teasing those who aren't part of the group, especially when they're not strong enough to stand up for themselves. Torgeir just backed down and kept more and more to himself."

She sat quietly looking out at the Skarstein Valley. Then she turned to Dag.

"They called him Midge," she said. "It got worse after you left. Most children are probably like that; they tend to pick on someone who doesn't have an older brother or a father to lean on—or to threaten with—I don't know."

Dag propped his elbow on the steering wheel and rubbed his eyes tiredly.

"I shouldn't have left," he said. "Then this might not have happened—maybe."

She responded mildly: "A man has to be where his work is. No one is at fault. Perhaps someday we'll find out what happened. It may be painful, but then we'll at least be sure there's nothing more to be done. In spite of everything it might prove to be a relief."

"Possibly. Maybe like an infected finger. An amputation hurts more, but at least the sore begins to heal."

"Yes," she said.

And later: "You can drive on now. But don't drive fast. We'll be home soon enough."

Polar Bear

One day the sun disappeared.

It had been overcast for a while, but this day it was completely clear. Torgeir stood by the shed sawing logs when he noticed a small slice of the sun peeping up over the lowest saddle of the island. Only seconds later it was gone.

He called the twins. They all watched as the snow on the rounded, rocky slopes turned to a deep, deep red. The shadows became tinted with dark violet. Bundles of light fanned out through the haze above the sea. They shot up over the hillside and paused there a moment, quivering as they turned paler and paler. In the end only dusk remained.

The children had seen the sun disappear before. Even at Andøya the sun was gone most of the winter. But none of them could recall that the days had grown shorter so quickly. The daylight didn't last much longer now than at Christmastime at home.

Torgeir was much more concerned about their getting out into the fresh air during the few hours of daylight. He himself had work to do. But the twins needed the change, and he let them play.

When the last traces of the sun's rays were gone, he went back to the woodpile. Terje and Lise were building a snowman. It was mild out, and the snow packed easily.

Suddenly Terje pointed towards the sound. "Wh——what, what is that?" he stuttered.

Lise followed his glance. "Oh my gosh," she exclaimed. "It must be a sheep."

Terje called out: "Something's coming across the ice, Torgeir. A sheep or something."

Torgeir straightened up and peered towards the sound. Almost that very second he dropped the saw and came running.

"Get in!" he yelled. "In! In!"

He herded them in front of him. The door slammed shut. He fell on the crossbar and fumbled with ten thumbs to get it in place.

When he turned around he was out of breath. His eyes were round as saucers.

"It was—a bear," he stammered.

"But, but—" Lise's eyes were just as big. "It was white —or yellow."

"Polar b——" Torgeir checked himself. But Terje had heard.

"Polar bear—sure. There aren't any polar bears in Norway, or are there?"

Torgeir didn't answer right away. He had sensed something that scared him almost more than the bear. A frightening thought crossed his mind: "Could it be that— we *aren't* in Norway?"

"Stand still!" he barked when Terje glanced towards the window. "We'll hear if it comes close. Don't be afraid. It can't get in."

Another white lie. Actually Torgeir was convinced that the bear could crush the door with a single swat of its paw. He had got into the habit of saying the opposite of what he meant.

Padding strides sounded in the snow outside.

They held their breath and didn't budge an inch.

How soft the strides were. The granular snow barely crunched under the animal's paws. For a while it was right by the door. It sniffed and snorted a few times, then shuffled off. The padding disappeared around back of the cabin.

Intuitively they withdrew further into the room and huddled together. For a long time they heard nothing and finally dared tiptoe to the window. They craned their necks and waited.

Then it came, rounding the corner of the house at a smooth, easy gait and wagging its head from side to side as if sniffing for something. Its shaggy body was large and bulky, but it moved with the grace and ease of a cat.

"Quiet!" whispered Torgeir, as if someone had moved or said something.

The bear was heading for the shore. It waddled calmly down the slope. Once, when it had almost reached the shoreline, it stopped and scented the wind with its pointed head stretched high in the air. Then it shuffled out onto the ice.

They watched for a long time. At the edge of a broad lane it plunged into the water with a splashing belly flop. The white head glided easily through the sea. Having crossed the crack it heaved itself onto the ice again with a mighty bound and loped on until the yellow-white colour was indistinguishable against the ice.

They let out their breath.

"Do you think it'll come back?" Lise whispered, her eyes and voice still brimful of excitement.

"No-o." Torgeir seemed to be thinking of something else. "It stays mostly on the ice, I think. Catches seals there."

"No, really—? Are there seals in Norway, too?" Terje tried a sarcastic smile. But he glanced questioningly at his brother.

Torgeir needed time to think. He leaned closer to the window and shaded his eyes, apparently trying to locate the bear. But actually something far more important was on his mind. The bear had revealed where they were.

All the pieces had fallen into place. The barren landscape, the darkness, the ice and driftwood, the kerosine drums—and now, the polar bear; everything indicated that they were farther north than they had thought. Further than the North Cape. Way up in the Barents Sea—on Svalbard.

The cabin was most likely a trapper's home in the hunting season. The trapper had gone. So had the sun. The long, dark winter was just around the corner. And they only had food for two or three more days.

Never had he been so close to giving up.

Still, reluctantly and rather laboriously, he launched into an explanation of how the ice in the Arctic Sea drifted with the current. It could be carried to Norway as well—to Finnmark anyway. And the polar bear—? Well, when the ice could make it, so could the polar bear—on very rare occasions.

To show that he was convinced they were out of danger, he unbarred the door and went to fetch the firewood he had sawed. But he didn't feel particularly confident. The tracks from the wide paws were alarmingly big, bigger than any footprints he had seen before. His eyes darted from side to side as he stepped stealthily across the snow.

At one point between the shed and the kerosine drums there was a jumble of tracks. The area was pockmarked with prints and the bear had pawed up a mound of snow.

Curiosity got the best of Torgeir. He went to take a closer look.

Obviously, the bear had been digging for something. Torgeir leaned over and caught sight of a grey patch that looked like cement in a depression in the bedrock. He forgot that he was afraid, dropped to his knees and started digging with his hands where the bear had left off. Little by little a cement wall came to view in the bedrock. In the middle there was a thick wooden trapdoor held in place by an iron bar. On one side hung a padlock.

Was it a well? But why should a well be padlocked? And why had the bear tried to get at it? Had it smelled something?

He remembered having seen a small black key in the kitchen cabinet. In a flash he was inside and found it. Terje and Lise were sitting by the stove talking. They were left dumbfounded when he dashed out again without saying a word.

The key fitted, but turned reluctantly in the icy lock. Torgeir gritted his teeth and twisted. At last the lock sprang open with a click.

And so did the trapdoor.

How could joy be expressed by such heartrending sobs? The sudden flow of tears was unstoppable. His eyes blurred. He barely had a chance to look at the precious treasure.

The dark hole behind the door was a food cellar. Inside was a room the size of a large packing crate, and on the concrete floor stood carton upon carton of food. He lay on his stomach and pored over the riches—cans of meatballs, stew, fishballs, soups—packages of all shapes and forms, some with inscriptions—smoked meat, salted meat, grouse, dried fish—food to last months, years maybe. There was no end to the wealth.

Later, when they were stuffing themselves with meatballs in thick gravy and eating more than was good for them, Terje remarked: "If that ol' bear comes back, I'll go out and thank him for dinner."

"Then he'll make a dinner out of you!" Torgeir laughed.

"Well—in any case we can leave some meat out for him. We've got enough of it now, haven't we?"

"Plenty," Torgeir said. "Enough to last us for months, half a year at least."

Their forks paused in mid-air. The twins stopped chewing and stared at him.

"What possible use could we have for all that?" asked Lise.

Faint Hope

"Myrmo! Move your plane! We're rolling out another one."

Flight Sergeant Myrmo sat in the cockpit of KKB and brought the log up to date. He had just test-run the engines.

"O.K.!" He waved to the mechanic who was shouting from the hangar door. "Bring the tractor. I'm coming."

"No, start up and get out of the way. We're in a hurry. The tractor's already hitched to KKG."

"Well, all right then." Myrmo settled into the pilot's seat and started the engines. He manoeuvred the aircraft in a wide arc out on the apron and swung it deftly into its new parking place. The whole operation was quickly done. Old routine. He cut the engines and grabbed again for the log.

When he had scribbled his initials in the last column and

snapped the book shut, he saw that the other plane was already in place. The tractor was on its way into the hangar again. The hangar doors rolled shut, and the apron was empty.

Myrmo ran a hand across his forehead. A shadow of a thought had crossed his mind, but he couldn't quite bring it into focus. The scene reminded him of something. KKG stood outside the hangar in almost exactly the spot he had taxied KKB from a moment earlier. That had happened before. Of course it had. There was nothing unusual about moving one aircraft away from the hangar doors to make room for another.

But what did he connect it with? A vague apprehension, something undefinable, had flashed by like a breath and was gone.

KKG? Empty apron?

The children!!

He held his breath. His eyes picked out the route they had taken after he had shooed them away from the air-craft—across the apron, along the south wall of the parachute shed and around back of the building. He hadn't seen them after that, neither on the road to the main gate nor in the fields behind it. Had they stopped on the other side of the parachute shed? When did they go on? And where?

Myrmo jumped suddenly out of the seat and ran to the door. He pounded down the two top steps of the ladder then leaped to the ground. Seconds later he stood in the hangar lounge, telephone in hand.

"Operations? Do you know where Captain Henriksen is? Can you get hold of him?"

He fidgeted nervously until he heard Henriksen's deep voice: "Yes."

"It's Myrmo. I have to talk to you. At once. It's terribly important."

"What about?"

"It has to do with—. No, wait—don't make me say it on the phone. It's equally important for you. If not more so. At once—please."

A short pause. Then a rumbling reply.

"Coming. By car."

"Fine. I'll be sitting in KKB on the apron. We have to be alone."

Myrmo took a smoke while waiting. He sat in the pilot's seat and kept an eye on the road to Skarstein Valley. Henriksen's grey Volvo came into view. It approached the squadron area at high speed, turned onto the apron and roared to a halt behind the aircraft. Myrmo drummed anxiously on the controls until Henriksen slumped into the seat beside him.

"O.K. Spit it out."

"Well, this isn't exactly easy. I've hit on something that may sound completely crazy. But it may not be—crazy, that is. It's about Captain Solheim's kids."

A spark appeared in Henriksen's eyes.

"The kids! Do you mean . . . ?"

"I mean—my God, it's so unlikely—but I mean there's an ever so small chance they might be alive."

Henriksen wasn't the kind who was easily rattled. But now he grabbed hold of the chair with both hands and leaned towards Myrmo.

"Out with it," he said, earnestly.

118

"All right, but don't take it for more than it's worth."

Myrmo pointed through the side window at KKG and explained: "I was standing over there checking the engines on KKB when the children came up. We talked about this and that, but as I've said before, they became very interested when I told them KKB was going to Sola. They wanted to go along to visit their father, and we know now why *that* was so important for them. Well—I sort of shrugged it aside by suggesting they ask their mother to have a talk with the station commander. We had plenty of room—it wasn't that—and the station commander might have given them permission. But there was all too little time. We were almost due to leave. Quite another matter was that they didn't *dare* go home. But I didn't know that then."

Myrmo pointed to the parachute shed. "They disappeared around the corner, and I didn't see them go any further. I warmed up the engines and moved KKB over here. At the same time KKG was towed out of the hangar and parked where it's standing now—precisely where KKB had been when I talked to the kids. I cut the engines and spent five or ten minutes securing everything in the back of the plane. When I returned to the hangar, both aircraft were ready and there was no one on the apron. A little later, we all went out together and started up. You flew to Half Moon Island, we to Sola."

Henriksen had paled. His hands shook as they gripped the armrests.

"You mean—you mean they might have decided to hitch a ride to Sola. And got on the wrong aircraft?"

"Yes."

There was a long, ghostly silence.

Then Henriksen got up. "Thanks a lot, Myrmo," he said. "I really think you may be right. I'll call Solheim at once. We must fly to Half Moon Island tomorrow."

He left Myrmo and went into the office of the chief technical officer, Captain Bakke. "Can I borrow your phone?" he asked.

"Sure." Bakke shoved the phone across the desk and pointed to a chair.

The switchboard operator gave Henriksen speedy service. She was a friend of his. It took only a few minutes. Dag was in.

"Captain Solheim speaking."

"Dag—this is Bjørn. If you're standing, sit down. Please sit quietly and listen without interrupting. There may, I said *may*, be a small hope—of finding the kids alive. No, no don't interrupt. It's only a faint hope, Dag. Very, very faint. But there is a chance. Now listen . . ."

Henriksen repeated almost word for word what Myrmo had told him. At the other end of the line Dag listened silently. Now and then he drew a quick breath that Henriksen could hear.

Having related Myrmo's story, Henriksen added on his own account: "At Half Moon Island we all went ashore together. We were in a hurry. Had to be off before dark and had a lot of equipment to load. But we left a lot behind, too. A good deal of food, among other things. If—as unbelievable as it may seem—if the children really went ashore thinking they were at Sola, they may have found the cabin—and may be there now."

Not a sound came from the other end.

"Hello? Are you there, Dag?"

"Yes—thanks, Bjørn. When are you leaving?"

"Tomorrow morning. There's not more than a half hour of light there now. Well, a kind of light, anyway. Dusk is more like it. Are you coming?"

"Yes. I'm coming. Tonight."

The Eleventh Hour

"In America they have submarines that go under ice," Terje said. "They're a half mile long. They punch a hole in the ice and come to the surface at the North Pole."

"Pooh," said Lise.

"Cross my heart. I saw one on TV. It shoved away the ice and popped up."

"Certainly not as thick ice as we have here."

"Much thicker. You think we're at the North Pole?"

"No—but no one comes here from America, anyway."

"It could happen. If someone calls and asks them."

"Who would do that?"

"The king—or somebody."

"Oh—"

Torgeir stood in the kitchen listening to the twins chatter in the other room. Obviously they, too, had begun to suspect that they were not in Norway. His little white lies might have become too transparent. But as long as they didn't ask, he let them believe what they wanted, and some small straw to cling to couldn't hurt them even though it was a figment of the wildest fantasy. He didn't quite know himself what to hope for. A helicopter, maybe. But he knew they couldn't fly as far as Svalbard. In any case a plane would come first.

It would soon be light.

The murky twilight in the middle of the day was now so short that they had to make good use of what little was left. In less than a week there would probably be no daylight at all, and the chances of being saved would lessen.

Torgeir was tense. He kept an eye on both his watch and the window. If Dad were to come at all, if he had finally guessed what had happened, he would gauge his flight so as to arrive while it was light.

Torgeir kept a kerosine can handy. It would take only a few seconds to set the bonfire ablaze.

He finished with the breakfast dishes and took a look out the window. The island was still clothed in darkness, but pale streaks of dawn had begun to inch their way down the mountainsides across the sound. The peaks stood in sharp profile against the sky.

"Get some clothes on and hurry outside," he called. He heard the twins bustling around the room. The door swung shut with a crash when he himself was almost dressed. He grabbed the key to the food cellar and was about to leave the house when he heard a bloodcurdling scream outside, first from Lise, then from them both.

There was terror in their voices. He threw himself at the door and stormed out. Without looking to either side he streaked off in the direction the sounds came from and found the twins halfway down the slope. They were standing close together and their cries drowned one another out. Not until he was almost at their side did he catch a word that made him freeze in his tracks and spin around.

"Bear! Bear!" they screamed in chorus.

The polar bear stood about fifty yards away, a huge bruiser with ragged, dirty-yellow fur. It craned its neck and sniffed in their direction with its pointed snout. Behind it stood a little white bundle, a tiny cub with a funny, curious-looking face. It cocked its head and gazed at them with large, wondering eyes.

But Torgeir hardly noticed it. He stared fear-stricken at the powerful mother bear.

With the little reason he still possessed after the paralysing shock, he realized that the way back to the cabin was blocked. They had the bears in front of them, behind them the ice-covered sound with its treacherous cracks and pockets of slush.

The big bear snarled and bared its teeth. Steam poured like smoke from its open mouth. It came a few steps closer, hesitated—and halted with all four paws planted firmly on the ground. It seemed horrendously large and its muscles bulged under the fur when it moved.

The twins had stopped screaming, but tried in vain to repress their sobs. Torgeir threw a glance over his shoulder and saw that Terje had his skis clutched firmly under one arm. He seemed to have been petrified in the same position as when he first saw the bear.

Torgeir felt hopelessly empty-handed. Would a ski be of

any help against a bear? He didn't think so, but he eased a few careful steps backwards all the same. Anything would be better than bare knuckles.

"Give me a ski," he whispered desperately to Terje. He reached a hand behind him and caught hold of the ski tip. Instantly he shifted his grip and swung the ski in front of him like a lance.

The bears watched him. They didn't budge.

Was there hope after all?

"Maybe they're not hungry," thought Torgeir. "Maybe they'll go away? Maybe they're afraid, too?"

Still he trembled so violently that the tip of the ski drew circles in the air. Had it not been for the twins behind him, he would have turned and fled, no matter where. It was almost unthinkable to remain standing in front of the glistening rows of teeth in those mammoth jaws.

However, the twins *were* behind him. There was no way past them.

The day was soon at its brightest. Nonetheless, it was murky, like a rainy, overcast day at home. But they were so close they could plainly see the bears' eyes. The big one followed their movements with undivided attention. The little one shifted its head from side to side, looking now at its mother, then at the strange creatures it had never seen before.

The cub was the first to grow impatient. Suddenly it padded past the mother and continued confidently towards the children. It looked friendly enough and probably wanted just to sniff at them to find out what kind of strange animals they were.

But the mother growled a warning, a vicious snarl that

left Torgeir's stomach tied up in knots. Lise fell to her knees in the snow and muffled her sobs with her mitten.

The cub stopped and looked back. Then, as if it couldn't care less, it padded on.

The mother followed with long, soft, almost silent strides.

Torgeir screamed. He bellowed with all his might at the she-bear's face. It was hard to tell whether the animals were frightened or simply taken aback. At any rate they stopped. The cub sat down and stared. But soon curiosity got the upper hand and it set out again. Its paws tripped even quicker across the snow. It looked like a rolling ball of cotton.

The mother followed. A wild roar ripped through the quiet air.

The roar penetrated deep into Torgeir's consciousness. It was the last stab of fear he registered. Something snapped inside him. He felt nothing, neither fear, nor courage—nor hope. His thoughts encompassed only a grim determination that the bears were not to get past him—no matter what.

He howled until his lips frothed. He tramped his feet in the snow and waved the ski menacingly. He swung it in front of him, slammed it against the ground, jabbed it at the cub and ran a few steps forwards, screaming at the top of his voice.

The little bundle turned tail and scampered back to its mother. The mother bear shoved it aside with a sweep of her snout. But she too stopped again, snapped at the air and eyed Torgeir with a snarling scowl. Barely twenty yards now separated them.

Deep inside, Torgeir had a feeling that the air was quivering and that the vibrations steadily grew in intensity as if a violent, thundering noise were drawing nearer.

But he wasn't conscious of anything other than what he was faced with. He saw the bear rear up on its hind legs and paw at the air. It seemed to be defending itself against an invisible attacker. Then suddenly it lunged around and fled across the snow with long, awkward bounds.

At the same time a deafening noise cascaded in on Torgeir's ears. It was as if the whole world collapsed. A black shadow flashed over his head, and he was toppled to the ground by a violent rush of air.

Scrambling on all fours he threw back his head and caught sight of an Albatross as it swerved unsteadily into a cloud of snow whipped up by the propellers.

Amid an inferno of sounds—the drone of engines, the bear's growls and the sobs of the twins—he heard his own squeaky voice:

"Dad! Dad!"

Operation Arctic

The Maritime Operations Centre in northern Norway was seemingly a chaotic jumble of men scurrying back and forth. They gave orders, received orders, wrote, telephoned, studied maps, measured, calculated, discussed and made decisions. But out of this chaos came a thoroughly considered plan for Operation Arctic.

Everyone involved had already been placed on standby. The naval patrol ship *Nornen* was docked at Hammerfest, her decks a beehive of activity as the crew rushed to get everything ready on time. At Bardufoss Air Force Base the ground crew of 339 Squadron was busy equipping a helicopter for arctic flying. They loaded tents, sleeping bags, fur jackets and food for three days in case the pilots should be forced to land on the ice. At Andøya an Albatross was already checked and put on two hours' readiness.

All units were waiting anxiously for the operation order.

It came through a little past midnight. The text was crisp and concise:

to: hms nornen, andøya air force base, bardufoss air force base.

from: maritime headquarters.

operation order no 1. nov 15 2350 hrs. execute operation arctic. aim: rescue three children from half moon island, svalbard. participating forces: hms nornen, 333 squadron, 339 squadron. procedure: 1 (one) helicopter is to be transported by hms nornen to the ice edge at 7520 degrees north 2300 east and will prepare to fly from there to half moon island. 1 (one) albatross is to survey the area checking weather conditions one hour before the helicopter is due for takeoff and will accompany the helicopter during flight to provide rescue, navigation and communication assistance. radio: frequency plan 2. weather: unstable, cloudy, low fog banks, light breeze. total darkness sets in nov 18. three-quarter moon most of the day. orders: helicopter lands on the ship's landing platform date/time 160500. helicopter fuel will be transported by truck from banak air station during the night. nornen weighs anchor 160700. estimated time of arrival at ice edge 170800. final phase begins as soon as conditions allow. albatross estimates arrival in the area at 170830 unless new orders are issued. confirm. end.

Everyone knew what to do. At the stroke of seven in the morning, the *Nornen* was ready and steamed out of the harbour at Hammerfest, following the inshore channel northwards. The weather was good. Not a ripple disturbed the mirror-smooth sea.

For the landlubbers on board, the three helicopter crewmen, the calm weather was a relief. The risk of high seas was the first thing they had inquired about when they stepped out of the helicopter after landing. None of them gave it a second thought when they had to fly through the turbulent winds that quite frequently tossed their aircraft around like a feather between the high mountains of northern Norway. But being on a rolling ship was something else. The very thought made them queasy.

The pilot was Lieutenant Fosse, a lean, sinewy fellow with a twinkle in his eye. Second Lieutenant Bryn, the co-pilot, had red hair and a temper to match. The third, whose name was Relling, was the flight mechanic. He was a large, solid and quiet character. His ears were prominent. They stood out like wings.

"He's good to have along in an emergency," Bryn explained to the *Nornen*'s skipper, Lieutenant Commander Brevik. "He can fly home for help."

They sat in the officers' mess aboard the ship and relaxed over a cup of coffee and a smoke. The day was almost over, and they were finished with their dinner. The Norwegian coast had long ago slipped below the horizon.

"This coffee is stronger than lye," Fosse remarked. "What's it made of?"

"Mostly coffee and water," Brevik replied. "You'll get used to it. But make sure you get here on time for coffee breaks. Our engineers steal it. Use it as rust solvent."

It was warm and quiet inside the mess. The monotone

throb of the engine and the rush of foaming water outside the portholes as the bow ploughed its way through the sea were already familiar sounds that went in one ear and out the other.

Lieutenant Commander Brevik had a beard and unkempt, curly hair. He also smoked a pipe with a crooked stem. It wasn't difficult to see he was a sailor. He seemed to be a serious young man who planned his end of the operation to the smallest detail.

"I'm afraid there's little I can do if you have to make an emergency landing on the ice," he said. "This isn't exactly an icebreaker."

"You can head home and get another helicopter," said Fosse. "We can manage a few days as long as we come down in one piece."

"And if not?"

"I guess all you'll find is a hole in the ice."

"How's that?"

"Well—" Fosse stroked his chin and shot a glance at Bryn and Relling. "If we are forced to land, it'll most likely be because the engine stops, which means we have to autorotate. We use the rotor like a windmill. It spins freely while we plummet downwards and the helicopter is manoeuvrable as long as it spins. If the air is clear so that we can use the landing light, we're home free. We can swoop to a halt just over the ice by using the energy from the windmill. But the timing has got to be perfect, because the rotor stops the moment we use it to brake with. Don't have a snowball's chance in Sahara if it's foggy. Can't see the ice before it hits us in the eye. Have no idea when to stop. If we brake too early we get left hanging in mid-air, literally. But not for long. The rotor quits and we plunge the rest of the way. If we brake too late, well—then we've plunged already."

"So fog is your worst problem?"

"Sure, sure. On foggy nights it's just hopeless. When we switch on the landing light it's like sitting in a dazzling pile of white suds."

"Hmmm," Brevik murmured. "Sounds fairly grim. Is there much chance of engine trouble?"

"Almost none. What I'm really afraid of is losing the Albatross in the dark. Without radar we haven't a ghost of a chance of finding either Half Moon Island or the *Nornen*. We'll simply run out of fuel while searching. That's when the engine stops—according to our experience."

Brevik chewed on his pipestem.

"But surely the Albatross will be able to find you on its radar if you lose sight of each other?"

"Of course. Mind you—it's no piece of cake to regain contact. Think of the danger of colliding in the dark. We have to be careful. The minutes slip away, and we haven't much more fuel than we need to get there and back."

Brevik clasped his hands behind his neck and leaned back. He puffed energetically on the pipe and studied Fosse through a cloud of smoke.

"I'm afraid we haven't much chance of success, then," he said. "Odds are there'll be fog along the way."

Fosse glanced at Bryn and Relling again. They said nothing—left it to him.

"A chance we might have to take," said Fosse. "It's risky to disappoint the kids, too, now that they know we've found them—and are waiting for us. If they lose their courage now, they could be in a bad way. The total darkness of a polar winter has taken its toll before. Of grownups."

Brevik agreed. "You're right, of course. There's little time to lose. We'll have to manage somehow—preferably tomorrow."

"Yes." Fosse looked at his watch and stood up. "As for me, I plan to hit the sack early. So I'll say goodnight now. We'll be awakened in good time before we reach the ice, won't we?"

"Early enough for a good breakfast," Brevik assured him. "We'll call you a little before the Albatross passes us on its way to check the weather."

It was Dag's Albatross that buzzed the *Nornen* the next morning. Henriksen was on board. He took over the co-pilot's seat as they passed the ship that had come to rest in a lane a few miles inside the ice edge. They radioed a greeting and promised to be back within an hour.

The weather was passable. They flew just under a cloud layer at two thousand feet, but except for some straggling fog banks drifting across the ice the air below them was clear. It wasn't completely dark. Moonlight filtered dimly through thin patches and breaks in the clouds and was reflected by the ice below. They glided alternately through twilight and murky shadows.

But worse lay ahead. About halfway they ran into fog. From a distance they could see it rising like a steep wall with peaks almost a thousand feet above the ice. The hope that it was just an isolated fog bank soon faded. They flew through the clear layer between the fog and the clouds, but the darkness around them deepened as the reflection from the ice surface disappeared. Minutes passed, but there was no change. A continuous sea of fog stretched as far as the eye could see.

Dag asked Henriksen to take over the controls. He needed a break to get over his disappointment. The first indications as they reached the ice had been so promising that he had expected the children soon to be safe and sound aboard the *Nornen*. Now the problems were piling up. The helicopter would hardly be able to land in the thick fog. It would be pitch dark near the ground, and landing lights would only make matters worse.

Pale and worried, he took in the foggy landscape that rolled and rolled out of the gathering darkness ahead.

"Chin up, Dag," said Henriksen. "There may be a clear layer near the ground. We'll have to go down on radar and take a look."

"Mmm-m." Dag nodded and considered how small the chances were, and how quickly a clearing could change and become thick as pea soup.

The thoughts remained unspoken. Over the intercom came the voice of the radar operator:

"Radar to skipper. I see land."

"Where?"

"Almost dead ahead. Seven—eight degrees port. Range forty nautical miles. Could be something like a chain of steep mountains."

"Edge Island." The navigator had joined in.

Dag fished the map out of a pocket under the side window and flicked on a light. Aside from the red glow that lit the instrument panel it was totally dark in the cockpit. His finger searched the map and zeroed in on Edge Island, which was located two or three miles north of Half Moon Island. It was only to be expected that the smaller island hadn't yet shown up on the radar screen. Low as it was, and snow covered as well, it would barely be distinguishable from the pack ice.

"Radar, let us know when you've got Half Moon Island on the scope."

"Sure."

Dag bit his lip. It was foolish to ask about such a routine matter. Impatience had made him edgy. He decided to let Henriksen stay at the controls for the rest of the trip.

It didn't take long before the radar operator was on the intercom again. He could make out the contours of the island. They were still a little hazy, but there was no doubt about where the island lay.

Henriksen looked over at Dag.

"I'll take her down. O.K.?"

"O.K., Bjørn."

Henriksen adjusted the mike and rumbled: "Pilot to crew. We're going on a little jaunt into this gravy. Lead me down to the surface a little south of the island, not too close, a quarter of a mile or so. We'll start the approach two miles to the east. Give me course and range."

"Radar here. Two miles it shall be. Turn starboard—steady—no, a little more—a little more starboard—there now, steady—steady . . ."

Ahead of them the moon had found a break in the ceiling and sent a quiver of rays through the air. But before they got there the gap had closed and the darkness seemed deeper than ever.

"Radar to pilot. You are two miles east of Half Moon Island now—now—now!"

"Course two six seven," the navigator intoned.

Henriksen banked sharply to the left. Gradually he cut back on the throttle, and spoke to Dag without taking his eyes from the instrument panel: "Twenty degrees flaps. Keep an eye on the radio altimeter and report when we get close to the ice."

Dag signalled thumbs up. He put out the flaps. Almost immediately small dots of fog began to streak by. Reflections from the navigation lights fanned out from the wing tips and were gone again. Then the fog sucked them in for good. The light glared more intensely on the panel.

"Port a little—steady. Range one mile."

"You sure you see the island clearly, radar?" Henriksen peered unhappily into the darkness. "Don't want to wind up plastered against some solid rock."

"No danger—you don't expect me to miss by a quarter of a mile, do you?"

"I've seen worse."

"Sure. But you're flying with 330 Squadron now."

It became almost pitch dark. Frost formed around the edges of the windscreen. The warning horn cut in to remind them that the landing gear wasn't down even though the engines were slowed almost to idling speed. Dag shut off the buzzer. They hadn't planned to use the wheels.

"Hundred and fifty feet," announced Dag. "Hundred and twenty—"

"How high can the ice blocks be?"

"Ten, fifteen feet. But we ought not go below fifty–sixty."

"Agreed."

Henriksen eased the stick back a little.

"Eighty feet—seventy—"

The engines roared to life. Centrifugal force shoved them deep into their seats and the climb-and-descent indicator levelled off at zero. They zoomed along at about fifty feet above the ice, but could see nothing.

"Quick—try the lights!"

Henriksen wasn't exactly on pins and needles. But he could remember times when he had felt a lot better.

Dag threw the switch. Immediately a blinding sea of light enveloped them. The beams bounced back from the fog and wrapped them in a dazzling white ball. They butted against a wall of light that blinded them even more than the darkness.

"Off!" shouted Henriksen.

He pulled the stick towards him and gave full throttle. The Albatross climbed rapidly to safe altitudes.

"They can't find us," Lise cried.

Torgeir closed the window. There was nothing more to listen for. The drone of engines had disappeared as quickly as it had come. The aircraft was on its way home. They had given up the search.

Outside the window a few coals glowed dimly on the bonfire. The damp sticks hadn't caught fire. When the plane came, Torgeir had rushed out with a can of kerosine and doused the wood with fuel. He had tossed a match on the logs, scampered inside, and watched from the window as the flames roared up—and died.

Lise was on the verge of tears.

"Will they come back?" she asked meekly.

"Don't be such a crybaby," Terje said, trying hard to muster courage.

Not more than a few minutes earlier they had been dancing and laughing with joy. Hope had come so suddenly. Their cheers resounded throughout the room. The flames from the bonfire cast a reddish glow on their ecstatic faces. But the joy faded along with the fire. Only ashes and disappointment remained.

The open window had let in the cold. Torgeir grabbed a chair and set it close to the stove.

"They'll be back." His tone of voice wasn't very convincing. "Probably not today, but tomorrow maybe."

He felt totally exhausted. The disappointment with the bonfire had been almost more than he could bear. So much work had gone into it and his expectations had been raised so high. But when it counted most, the fire had failed.

He knew why. It was he who had failed. Fear had made him careless. Even while pouring kerosine on the damp logs he thought he could feel the polar bear breathing down his neck. No matter how many times he told himself it was just his imagination, the feeling persisted. It was the first time he had dared go outside since the Albatross had scared away the bear, and the terror of that nightmarish moment was still with him. No power on earth could get him outside again—unless it was a matter of life and death.

Torgeir didn't know about the fog. He could see almost nothing outside and thought it was the black night that kept the pilots from finding the island. And he knew it wouldn't be light again until spring.

"We have to build a new fire," said Terje.

What he really meant was *you*. Torgeir knew he had to go out alone. He shivered despite the penetrating warmth from the stove.

"I'll go out and build it," he said. Inside him something protested. So he said it again.

"I'll build a superfire. So big they'll be able to see it from—from Norway!"

He didn't know how close to the truth he was.

Terje fetched the outdoor lantern and lit it while Torgeir put on his jacket, cap, scarf and mittens. When ready, he took the lantern from Terje and trundled out the door.

On the way to the shed he repeated over and over to himself: "Come on. Come on." Perhaps he was trying to persuade his feet to continue. It seemed as if they wanted to go in another direction. While his body leaned into the task, his feet dragged reluctantly behind and were ready to retreat at a moment's notice.

Twice he turned a complete circle to see if he was alone. Which he was—within the small circle of light from the lantern. He had now become aware of the fog, but had no idea how thick it was. The lantern cast rays about three or four yards away. Beyond that it was coal black. He struggled in vain to avoid thinking about the unseen horrors that might be lurking behind that black boundary.

The pile of driftwood had diminished significantly since they had begun to cut into the supply. But there were still plenty of logs left, enough for a huge fire.

He had to set the lantern down while he hauled the heavy

logs across the snow. He tugged and pulled until he reached the rim of the circle of light. Then he ran back for the lantern and carried it a bit beyond the logs. Time and again he went through this routine with feverish urgency. When a log was in place he went to get a new one.

Sweat poured from his face. But he didn't allow himself a single break before he was satisfied that the heap of logs was big enough. Then he tossed his jacket and scarf near the cabin wall and turned to the kerosine drums. This time he wanted to have a good supply of the fuel. The can wouldn't do. He wanted a drum.

He chose the one with the spigot. They had tapped it for some time and the remaining liquid splashed when he rocked it. He managed to lug the heavy container down from the rack and had no difficulty rolling it down the slope to the bonfire. At one point it gathered speed and rolled away from him, veering off to one side. In chasing after it he wound up outside the circle of light and thought immediately he heard something behind him. His feet wanted to race for the cabin door, but he overcame the urge.

"There's nothing there. There *isn't*," he assured himself.

The drum had come to rest against a rock. Torgeir ran back for the lantern, lifted it above his head and swung it threateningly towards an unseen foe. Animals were afraid of fire. He had read that somewhere. But there was only scant comfort in the thought.

He struggled on till he reached the bonfire. Once there he put his shoulder to the drum and rolled it onto the heap of logs. Some of them shifted and the drum rolled to a standstill.

At last everything was ready. All he had to do was open the spigot and the kerosine would gush onto the logs. It would be a gigantic blaze.

Suddenly he itched to get inside. Not a moment longer did he want to stand in the threatening dark. He grabbed the lantern, raced for the door, tore it open and ducked inside. Frantically, he threw the bar in place as if he had just escaped some mortal danger.

Unsuccessful Attempt

"Helicopter to Albatross. I'm ready for take-off. Over."

"Fine. We're waiting. The clear layer is between one and two thousand feet. Level off at fourteen hundred and stay due north. We'll find you."

Lieutenant Fosse hit a switch. The low hum of the start motor shifted almost unnoticeably to the intense whine of the jet turbine. The rotor began to turn and picked up speed. Soon the low and muffled flop-flop became quick and sharp as the crack of a whip.

"Ready?" Fosse took a tighter hold of the controls.

"Ready," said Bryn.

"Ready," acknowledged Relling from the back seat.

After one last look at the tachometer Fosse shoved the left pedal almost to the floor and pulled up the pitch control. The helicopter rose vertically from the platform, hesitated a moment, and slipped sideways into free air.

They climbed quickly towards the rendezvous point. The pack ice seemed vaguely iridescent. It stretched like a grey surface beneath them with silvery spots where the moon shone through. Behind them was the *Nornen* looking like a trimmed Christmas tree in the endless expanse of ice.

There was a dry crackle in Fosse's headphones.

"We have you on the scope," came Dag's voice through the ether. "Proceed on course till we have your lights in sight. We'll inch carefully in. How close do you want us?"

"A hundred yards so long as the visibility holds," answered Fosse. "Later we may have to make do with twenty."

Whether the words were jinxed or whether Fosse had keen foresight shall remain unsaid. At any rate they were only yards apart a half hour later. From the cockpit of the helicopter they had only the three dots of light to show them where the Albatross was—green and red on the wing tips and a brighter white on the tail fin. Sometimes, when they flew through free-floating patches of fog and the lights faded to a smouldering glow in the dark, it became almost impossible for Fosse to judge the distance between the helicopter and the aircraft. He had to make Bryn responsible for keeping the lights in view while he himself flew blind, relying entirely on the instruments. But at the same time he had to be constantly on guard to avoid colliding or flying into the dangerous backwash from the Albatross's propellers.

Only once did the teamwork fail. They got caught up in the turbulent backwash and had for a moment the terrible impression that they had lost half the rotor. It bounced and lurched so violently that Fosse lost control, and the helicopter shook, wobbled and careened through the air like a wing-shot bird. When Fosse finally regained control and manoeuvred away from the eddies, the Albatross was nowhere to be seen. Several nerve-racking seconds passed in which they had no idea whether they were still perilously close to the aircraft.

"We lost you," Bryn said over the radio.

Henriksen answered: "O.K.—stay on course."

"We can't see the ends of our noses."

"So what? Just hold your course. We'll descend and stay a bit lower than you. Proceed on course."

"Check."

Almost a minute went by.

"Can you see me?" Henriksen queried.

"No—thick as soup."

"Wait—it's beginning to thin out, I think—Yes, it's clearer here now."

"Altitude?"

"Twelve hundred and forty."

"We're at twelve hun—. Hey, there you are. We seem to have straggled a bit. Coming."

"Good boy. Hang on. Our navigator says only twelve more minutes."

Both Fosse and Bryn were sweating. The lights on the Albatross pitched up and down. Either the aircraft or the helicopter was undulating—most likely both. It made little difference. More than ever they felt comforted at having the plane so near and knowing there was a navigator aboard who had an idea of where they were.

The panel lights shone in front of Fosse, a tiny glow for each instrument. His eyes did not rest for a second, but shifted from the Albatross to the panel and back again. Among the luminous pointers were many that had to be pointed at just the right mark. But one was more important than all the others. He took his eyes off it for only seconds at a time. The air speed indicator had to read exactly a hundred and ten knots. That was the least the Albatross could stay airborne on, and the most the helicopter could do. There was no margin for error, none to mention at any rate. The blades of the rotor were on the verge of stalling and Fosse tried not to think of the acrobatics it would perform if they began pushing a hundred and fifteen. He had enough to worry about as it was.

"How's it going, Fosse?" Henriksen's soothing voice broke through the clatter of the rotor.

But Fosse had no time for conversation. "Mind your own business," he snapped. "If you distract me, I'm likely to take a hunk out of your tail before you know it."

"True, true," Henriksen answered with unruffled calm. "Can't really get my mind off that buzz saw of yours, you know. But luckily it'll soon be over. We have Half Moon Island clear as day on the scope. Wait a minute—."

They sweated and waited. Aside from a few moonlit clouds there was nothing to indicate that the last phase of the operation would be any more pleasant than it had been so far. A proper break in the clouds and a splash of bright moonlight would have helped some. But it had to come soon. Their fuel supply didn't allow for any delays.

It was Dag's turn to speak when the carrier wave once more buzzed in the headphones. "Fosse—listen closely. In precisely two minutes we'll break visual contact with you and climb to two thousand feet. We'll remain there and follow you on radar. You'll be given courses till you're right above the cabin and—well, you'll have to decide for yourself from there. Continue on course when we break away. At that point you'll have three minutes flying time left. O.K.?"

"O.K."

Fosse muttered to Bryn and Relling: "You think he expects us to go down in this soup?"

"He's hoping, of course," said Relling.

Fosse tasted the thought.

"Well—we can always give it a try. But if it's just as thick all the way down, we'll have to come up again quick as lightning. We're no help to the kids if we arrive as ground beef."

"Feel sorry for them," Bryn said. "They can hear us now."

The lights on the Albatross were gone. Fosse dimmed the panel lights until he could just barely check the instruments. The details in the cockpit were tinged with a pale rosy cast.

As their night vision improved they could see the fog layer beneath them. It was compact, without a single break. There was no chance of worming their way down through a hole.

They searched so intensely for a clearing that they started when the radio operator called them from the Albatross: "Helicopter from Albatross. You're almost there. Turn ten degrees port—steady—fine—keep your course."

There was a pause. Then: "You are directly over the cabin—now—now, *now*!"

Fosse put the helicopter into a tight turn and glanced down. Nothing had changed. One place was as good—or bad—as the next. They could just as well go straight down.

"Albatross." He spoke into the mike and at the same time pulled out a large handkerchief with which he wiped the sweat from his eyes. "Have you checked the air pressure against the radio altimeter?"

"Yes—set your altimeter at two nine point eight nine inches. So you're going down?"

"We'll have a go at it. But don't get your hopes up."

"No. Good luck!"

The helicopter was already spiralling in wide circles towards the fog. Fosse leaned involuntarily forwards and took a tighter hold of the controls. Not that it helped any. He neither saw better nor flew better. Most likely he was following an age-old instinct, perhaps a holdover from a time when man had to defend himself by simple means— hunched over to protect the body and with a tight grip on his spear or club.

The fog closed around them. It was like diving into a dark pool. The darkness deepened with each yard. But Fosse didn't notice. For him everything was happening inside the cockpit. The helicopter's movements in relation to the ground were registered and described from one moment to the next by the turn-and-bank indicator, artificial horizon, altimeter and vertical speed indicator. The meter hands swirled. Everything went very quickly. But there was still time. For a few seconds more he could let everything be—in the hope that Relling or Bryn would cry out that the fog had lifted.

"Two hundred feet," said Bryn.

Black night against the plexiglass screen.

"Hundred and fifty."

"Hundred."

"Landing light. Quick! Quick!"

Fosse pulled the stick in to his stomach and the clattering of the rotor shifted tone.

For one second the lights were on. That was enough. Bryn switched them off again before being given the order. It served no purpose to have them on.

Fosse shook his head in disappointment. It would have been indefensible to go lower. He was responsible for more than the helicopter and himself—for Bryn, whose face now matched the colour of his hair, and for Relling, who sat silent as a mummy in the seat behind them. The attempt had failed. They had to go up again.

He had no right to play with death.

Final Phase

The clamour of the helicopter's rotor just over the cabin
sent the kids again into ecstasy. It happened so quickly
that Torgeir hadn't even had time to throw on his jacket
and run out to light the fire. Now they thought it un-
necessary. Any moment the helicopter could appear out
of the dark and land.

So much deeper was their disappointment when the
clatter subsided and faded away. Once more it had
happened. Even the helicopter hadn't found them. It had
been so close. But the bonfire hadn't been lit. The hapless
bonfire was never lit at the right moment.

Torgeir pulled on his boots and ran out with the lantern
dangling from his hand. He flicked open the tap on the
kerosine drum, let the fluid run a while and heaved the
lantern into the fire so hard that the glass splintered. As
he ran towards the cabin he felt a puff, like a warm breath,

and saw dancing yellow lights reflected on the cabin wall.

He turned a moment in the doorway. The flames licked hungrily at the logs and rose high into the air. Night became light as day. But he saw how thick the fog was. It would take a huge bonfire. And now it looked as if it finally would be big enough.

He closed the door—which saved his life.

The next moment a deafening boom ripped through the air. The windowpanes shattered and pieces of glass tinkled across the floor. The walls creaked. A holocaust of flames and sparks climbed skywards outside the cabin.

"The drum!" was Torgeir's first confused reaction. Had it exploded?

Shock more than the air pressure had thrown him up against the wall. He dropped to his knees and rubbed a sore shoulder while his eyes searched feverishly for the twins. They were sitting on the floor. Why and how they had got there was something neither they nor he could explain. Their eyes were wide open with fear. They gaped as if ready to make one final scream from the threshold of nothingness. But not a sound came out. Time seemed to be standing still—as when a film unexpectedly stops and the last picture still lingers on the screen.

"Don't be afraid!" Torgeir screamed without noticing the fearstricken tone of his own voice. "It was just the kerodrum—kerodri—sine drum. It exploded."

The information didn't increase the twins' confusion, but didn't exactly clear it up, either. They came slowly to their senses and a new, more real fright washed over them. "The house is on fire!" howled Lise and jumped up.

"Fire! Fire!" shouted Terje as if he had the fire department on the line.

They rushed to the door and fumbled with the crossbar, but Torgeir managed to stop them just as the door swung wide open.

The cabin wasn't on fire. But the bonfire was a crackling, sputtering inferno. Burning logs had been thrown yards away. The drum had been split in two and lay in the middle of a hissing column of flames that rose fifteen feet into the air. The heat was so intense they had to turn their backs to the fire.

Torgeir shoved the twins back into the room and closed the door. Afterwards he just stood there, leaning his forehead against the doorframe. All at once he was tired, so tired.

Behind him Terje was explaining something very important to Lise.

"Now—" he said. Then his voice cracked. "Now—" He coughed to clear his throat. "Now at least they've—" Again his voice cracked and shifted to falsetto.

"Seen us!"

And he was right.

"Good God," said Fosse. "What was that?"

A beam came shooting up through the fog as if someone had turned on a giant searchlight. Under them the fog turned a bright, bluish white in an area that expanded rapidly, crested and began to shrink again. The colour faded through the spectrum from white to yellow to orange to red. There it held, a round spot with a faint, but clear reddish tint.

Bryn hadn't answered yet. He stared in disbelief at the strange light. At last he spoke: "It must have been an explosion."

"You said it. Something happened down there."

Fosse jammed the pitch control all the way to the lowest stop. The helicopter plunged into an autorotation glide and dropped like a lead weight.

"We're going down there now," Fosse shouted. "Even if we have to land in a mass of flames. Hang on tight!"

They spun in narrow circles through the pink-coloured fog. This time at least they had something to guide them. As long as the fog glowed around them, they knew they were on target. Hopefully there would be time to brake before they ploughed into the source of the light.

Fosse had one arm free after having left the pitch control in the bottom position. He zipped open his jacket and tugged his shirt open at the neck. The button popped against the plexiglass and rolled to the deck.

His eyes stayed glued to the instrument panel. He knew that Bryn would shout out if they lost the cone of light and strayed into the darkness. He would also hear from Bryn or Relling if they caught sight of the fire, or whatever it was that illuminated the fog.

They plummeted past five hundred feet. He was tempted to check the rate of descent, but let it go. In autorotation he could hold tighter circles and run less risk of losing the light cone. They had to hope for the best.

Had he made the right decision?

If not, he would probably never know. Nor would Bryn. Nor Relling.

He had perhaps ten seconds in which to change his mind. Eight seconds. Six—.

He gripped the stick tighter.

Then Bryn screamed as if—or rather, because—their lives were at stake.

"There it is! The fire! There! There!"

A quivering index finger pointed out the direction. Fosse shifted his gaze instantly from the instrument panel to a clearly visible red spot in the fog.

He pulled hard at the pitch control and they sank heavily into their seats as the speed decreased. The altimeter stopped spinning and they glided quietly towards the flickering point of light.

Still they saw nothing but the fire.

"Where's the cabin?" Fosse called. His unsettled nerves jumped at the thought of crashlanding on the only roof on the island.

Relling tapped him on the shoulder.

"I think I see it," he said in Fosse's ear. "Fifteen yards from the fire. To the right."

"Fine."

Suddenly the air cleared. Heat from the fire had driven the fog away. As if by the wave of a magic wand everything within the circle of light came into view—the cabin, the shed, the kerosine drums and the scattered, burning logs.

The helicopter hit the ground with a soft thump.

They sat perfectly still and caught their breath while the rotor lost speed and came to rest with a long, subsiding sh-sh-i-i-u-uh. Afterwards the only sound was the crackling of the fire.

But then the cabin door burst open and slammed against the wall with a crash.

Fosse jerked his head up and took a deep breath. He fumbled for the radio button, glancing up as if expecting to see the Albatross overhead. But the fog and darkness lay between. Only the radio waves bound them together.

"Alba—harumph—tross," he barked. "I've landed."

His tongue was bone dry and his heart pounded in his throat.

"Your kids are here, Captain Solheim," he said thickly. "Right now they're doing some kind of war dance outside the cockpit—or maybe a new version of shake—'fraid this isn't exactly my field."

When he received no answer, he added: "There's three of them—that's about what you were missing, isn't it?"

There was a pause.

At last an answer came through from somewhere in the darkness above. But the voice was Henriksen's: "Captain Solheim seems satisfied with the inventory. But don't talk so much. Get them aboard and bring them home."

"Why, yes. There's a good idea. By golly, I'll do it."

Fosse flashed a broad grin at Bryn and Relling.

Then he pulled the sliding door open and jumped out onto Half Moon Island.